Tyrone Gibbs
Trgibbsjr68@yahoo.com

Hey Sadie Watlington Rogers!
Thanks for supporting my 1st novel.
Keep your eyes open for my future
releases. I hope you Enjoy!

TR Gibbs

07-03-2020

INNOCENT, UNTIL PROVEN BLACK

by

Tyrone R. Gibbs, Jr.

All glory and thanks to God.

This book, based on true events, is dedicated to the
following:
To my beautiful wife, Shai-- Thanks for making me keep my
promise.
To my Mama, Chyrese—Thanks for giving me love, life, and a
lifetime of good advice.
To my Family and Friends-- Thanks to each of you for all your
support and for putting up with me.
To my Brothers and Sisters who served in combat-- Thanks
for your sacrifices to keep us all safe and Free!

Horsemen...Forever

A small group of soldiers sat quietly, their attention focused on two fighter jets streaking to annihilate a column of enemy tanks. Machine guns rattled in an impotent rage to stop the deadly aircraft. Great billows of smoke and fire exploded to life, like giant popcorn, as tank after tank was blown away. The planes flew out of sight as artillery rounds landed dangerously close to a hut being used as an aid station.

Inside the small building, dust and debris rained down on the occupants as man-made thunder rumbled outside. A lone medic made a futile effort to shield the open wounds of the casualties strewn about, but they were simply too many. He coughed as he waved a path through the swirling cloud of dust, making his way to one of his guys. The man was missing both legs.

"Doc!" the man called when he saw the medic's face. "I'm busted up pretty bad. You know what to do. Go ahead, I'm done. No use waistin' your time on a corpse that

ain't got the sense to just die! Hit me, Doc,
but promise me you'll tell my wife...tell my
wife...to go to hell! Cheatin' tramp! You let
her know, those were my dying words. God
bless the U.S.!"

"God bless you, Sarge. You saved the
platoon. Here, take this," said the medic, as
he injected him in what was left of his leg.
"Rest easy, Sarge."

"Doc! It's so cold! It's so..." **BOOM!**
The man's words were cut off by an
explosion. Outside, men were calling for
the medic as they began to dig franticly
through the rubble that was formerly a
shelter for first aid.

"Here he is!" one of the men yelled. The
medic was pinned beneath a wooden beam.
Blood trickled from the corner of his mouth.
As his friends lifted the beam, violins began
to play and...a phone rang. **RRIIINNGG!**

"Go get the phone, Simmonds!" barked a
man in the group seated before the TV.
RRIIINNGG! The others in the audience
groaned in disappointment as the phone
rang again, drowning out the sounds of

battle and the rescue of the medic on-screen.

"Alright, I'll get it! Press pause," Simmonds said as the medic was being pulled into a clearing.

"Screw you, answer the phone!" **RRIIINNGG!**

Okay, don't pause it, I've already seen it anyway, he thought. "That's alright! I hate the next part, anyway! Doc dies, but the Sarge makes it! He gets bionic legs and he goes home to kill his wife." **RRIIINNGG!** "Yeah, he's gonna be in the sequel." The men watching the movie began cursing at Simmonds as the medic gave his dying speech to the camera.

At the front desk, Simmonds answered as the phone began to ring again. **RRIII!** "Headquarters, Victory Company, Private Simmonds speakin', may I help you?" He prepared to take a note as the female on the line began to speak. Even at this hour of the night, an important call could be expected from higher headquarters. A look of disgust, much like the ones the spectators in the TV room made when he spoiled the movie, took over Simmonds' face and he tossed the pen in the air. He didn't care where it landed because he didn't need to write down an urgent message. The female on the phone, like most of the *callers tonight, was looking for her boyfriend. I should tell her he ain't here, so I can see the end of the movie. It's lucky for her he's my roommate. Plus, I've already seen this picture twice before.*

"Hold on, I'll get him for you," he mumbled into the phone. "Vas?" the female asked. It was German for, "What?" "Hold…on…ein…momen-tay…itch…vill…go…git…himmm…fo-wer… you-u-u!" <u>Dumb bitch</u>, he thought as he put the phone on the desk. <u>Learn English</u>, he advised in his head. "Hey, SGT Wickett, I'm goin' upstairs. Watch da desk!"

As Simmonds turned to the stairwell, a voice drifted from the TV room, "Why, does it do tricks?"

Simmonds started for the stairs, pausing as he thought he heard someone behind him say something about a redneck. He shook his head and continued upstairs, thinking, *everybody in the Army is a comedian! I mean, every nigger in the Army is a comedian! Or was that, every nigger is in the Army? Haw, haw, haw. Naw, most of 'em are in jail. Jail or the Army, great place to be for a nigger! They're too sorry to get a real job. As soon as I get out, I'm goin' back to Jimmy's. Now, he'll let me work on the cars, and not just clean the garage. Least I got a plan, not like these gangbangers. All they think about is...bangin'! Haw, haw. Stupid schnitzleheads, I don't know why they want brothers. German girls must have nigger in 'em. Maybe 'Nazi' means, 'nigger.' Haw, haw, haw.*

Simmonds continued walking upstairs, thinking, *man, I thought I was gonna git some sleep tonight but I guess I'll be runnin' a datin' service. Hell with that! This is the last time I fetch a nigger to the phone for a fraulein, tonight. And this 'un only 'cause it's for Eiric. He's the only black guy you can trust 'roun' here. Well, maybe not trust, but at least I like him. He's not like the others. Not like that loud mouth friend of his, Gandhi. He's probably in the room right now, with the rest of his posse. A buncha yard apes, hootin' an' hollerin', tearing up stuff and drankin' forties. Those gorillas better not be messin' with my stuff. A room fulla gorillas...now that's somethin' to talk about back home.*

Simmonds continued up the stairs, upset over being on duty while his bedroom was being "overrun" by people he didn't like.

Upstairs, in room 433, a small party was going on. Four men were seated before a TV, laughing and drinking sodas. A large man wedged into a bean bag was apologizing to the others. "I'm sorry, Fellas! Y'all know these things give me gas! I couldn't hold it any longer."

A man with glasses responded first, between chuckles, "Greasy, everything gives you gas!"

"Damn skippy!" yelled a skinny guy seated closest to Greasy. "Why didn't you get up and leave the room, Man?"

"I couldn't get up out of Eiric's stupid bean bag," Greasy replied.

"Oh, so now my bean bag is stupid because you couldn't get your big ass up? I didn't tell you to sit on it. You always sit on that thing..."

"And you always get stuck!" said the man with the glasses.

"Damn skippy! Then we have to pull you up! I swear, Greasy, you're the fattest man in the Army! Be all you can be, not eat all you can eat!" The others started laughing.

"Skippy, you're the skinniest man in the Army!" Greasy shot back. "You so damn skinny, your girl gave you a blowjob and flossed her teeth at the same time!" Skippy smiled and nodded his head while the other men laughed even harder. Finally, Skippy spoke.

"That's alright, that's alright. Just let me know when yo momma wants to floss again." The room exploded in loud outbursts of, "Ooooh!"

"Oh, you want to bring mommas in this?" Greasy asked. Before he could continue, the skinny man interrupted.

"That's right! I'd like to bring your momma in here, but, I can't move her big ass, and we all know, ain't no way in hell she's gonna fit in here, anyway. Well, maybe if we move all the furniture out. And knock out a wall. And put Vaseline around the door sill. And put a piece, I mean, a **whole** chocolate cake in the corner. Maybe **then** we could get her in here!"

Greasy rocked back and forth in the bean bag, reaching for Skippy as he tried to force himself to stand. His face was twisted into a murderous scowl. That's when Eiric stepped in between them.

"Big Greasy! Cool out! Don't eat him; we need him in case we go to war again! The enemy will take one look at that scrawny rascal, feel sorry for us and give up! Chill!"

Greasy's hardened face eased and he said, "I ain't gone hurt him 'cause I don't want to deal with his family. Hey, Gandhi, you saw that picture of all those people at his family reunion?" The man with the glasses nodded, still laughing at his friends.

"Yeah, all them scrawny motherfuckers. His family portrait looks like a bar code!"

"A bar code?" Gandhi said, "Damn!" then he started crying with laughter as he held his glasses in place. Eiric was already on the floor holding his side and trying to breathe.

Skippy laughed out loud, the loudest in the room, as he held his hand out to Greasy. Greasy had a huge grin on his face, obviously pleased with the success of his joke. He extended his arm and slapped Skippy's palm three times. On the third slap, they clasped hands for a few seconds. They then slowly pulled their hands away, keeping contact until their fingertips met. Each man curled his fingertips locking their hands in place a second longer. They released their hands and each one snapped their fingers. With the snapping sound, all four men yelled, "Horsemen!"

Simmonds had just reached the room as Skippy and Greasy had finished clapping hands. He was reaching for the doorknob when the four men yelled out their call sign. Simmonds shook his head thinking,

'Horsemen?' Gorillas, I say. If they're on my side of the room, I tell you what! Simmonds turned the knob and opened the door. He stood in the doorway and surveyed the room for a split second before entering.

He saw Stone, the skinny one they called "Skippy," seated on a hardback chair. Reynolds, or "Big Greasy," was being swallowed by Eiric's bean bag. Simmonds hated that bean bag and had secretly cut a hole in it. He then complained to Eiric about the mess it made, hoping one day he would throw it out. So far, his plan failed.

He then looked at Portland who was sitting on Eiric's bed, adjusting his glasses as he glared back at him. *Ain't that a surprise, old big mouth, Gandhi, leading a ruckus? Well, I see the ring leader and two of his flunkies, but where is Eiric? I know he didn't leave them in here with my sh...oh, there you are.* Eiric lifted his head off the floor as Simmonds stepped in the room. Simmonds looked at Eiric and smiled as he said, "What's up guys? Lesson, you got a call downstairs on line one."

"Who is it? Is it stateside?"

"Naw, it's a German chick."

"What's her name, Simmonds?"

"I didn't ask and she didn't say!" *Stop being a wad and go answer the phone.* "You want me to go talk to her for you."

"No thank you. Who did she ask for?"

"You."

"I mean, what name did she ask for? I'll know who it is if I know who she asked for."

"Cat Daddy!" Greasy exclaimed.

"Damn skippy!" said Skippy, agreeing with his friend.

Simmonds rolled his eyes and said, "She asked for, 'Eiric Lesson in 433.' That **is** you, right?"

"Aw, it's Gabe. I don't want to talk to her."

Gandhi looked at Eiric and spoke. "Man, you gotta talk to her sooner or later. She knows you're short. You can't just leave Germany and not at least say something to her. Fool, that girl is in love with you. Go on, Man!"

"Yeah, you're right. I just hate saying goodbye." He got up and headed to the door thinking, *I know Simmonds doesn't*

really like them being in here unsupervised.
"Yo, Sim, watch the room while I'm downstairs. Make sure they don't mess with my soda."

"No problem," Simmonds responded. "Just tell SGT Wickett I'll be down when you're finished."

Eiric agreed as he closed the door behind him. He walked slowly in the hallway toward the stairs. This was a call he had been putting off for weeks. He had successfully avoided Gabe for almost a month as his contract was coming to an end. A few more weeks and he would be back stateside, back in "the World," and he had hoped to get away without making any promises he couldn't keep or breaking any hearts. Hers or his own.

Back in room 433, a different kind of party was beginning. Gandhi watched from his seat on Eiric's bed as Simmonds walked over to his side of the room. He sat at a desk, facing the three other men, but his attention was on his personal space. From the corners of his eyes he could tell that everything was just the way he had left it this morning when he started duty. Charge-of-Quarters was a duty that lasted 24 hours, an eternity away from the things that provided him comfort and a taste of home.

After pushing his glasses up on the bridge of his nose, Gandhi spoke. "My man, Simmonds! You got the big 'Q' tonight. And you have it with SGT Wickett? Aw, Man, I feel sorry for you." *Redneck!* "SGT Wickett will have you getting busy all night." *I wish he could make you pick some cotton.* "By midnight, you'll feel like a slave." *Look at him, I bet that's killing him. He has to listen to a black man giving him orders all night.* "Pick up that, clean this, go get that phone." *Yeah, it's eating him up. He's turning red already.*

Naw, nigger! "Naw, Portland, SGT Wickett is alright." *As niggers go, not like you, you big mouth jigg.* "He said I could crash after everybody's sleep, maybe around two o'clock. After I make sure the common area is clean." *I gotta clean up after you slobs. That ain't right!*

Awww, he's gotta clean up behind us. I oughta really go mess up down there! "Oh, that's cool, Man. At least you'll get a few hours of sleep tonight." *I wonder what you'll dream about...lynching somebody, probably.* "But I thought you had duty with," *your redneck buddy,* "SGT Preston."

"I did, but he paid," *that nigger buddy of yours,* "SGT Wickett to work for him tonight." *How could he do that to me? Now, I'll have to listen to jungle music tonight. Thanks a lot, SGT Preston. I want my Billy Jo Bob album back since you made me work for that colored sumbitch.*

"If you pay me," *$2,000,* "I'll work the rest of the night for you." *So you can protect your precious hillbilly shit.*

"I ain't payin' you." *I'll buy you though, you fuckin' runaway!* "I'll do my own work," *with that nigger,* "and I won't complain about it, like some people do." *And I won't sang no nigger spirituals while I'm doin' it! Swing low, sweet...*

"What do you mean, 'Some people?' What 'people' are you referring to?" *Say it! Say it! I know you want to call me a nigger so bad! Just say it! Fix your mouth like you're about to say it! I wish this motherfucka would say it! I will fuck him up! Motherfuck getting in trouble!*

What the hell is this uppity jigg talking about? Simmonds thought as fear slipped into his body. He swallowed noisily before speaking. "I mean, **some people** bitch about working on CQ, that's all." Simmonds tried to hide the fear building inside him. *Why couldn't this be just me and him? I would kick his black ass back to Harlem! But I can't stop Big Reynolds. That boy is huge and strong as a mule! If it was just me and you, Gandhi, I tell you what!*

"Calm down, Portland! Why do you always have to make everything about race? I didn't say, 'You people,' I said, 'Some people.' That could be anybody." Simmonds managed a smile, proud that he had made Gandhi look bad by taking the high road first.

Gotcha, redneck! "What makes you think I was being racial?" *You fucking Klansman!* "I didn't say anything about race, did I?" he asked Skippy and Greasy. They both shook their heads and looked Simmonds in his twitching eyes.

With some effort, Greasy pushed himself out of the bean bag and Simmonds responded by stepping back in a defensive stance. Greasy growled, "What, you gone hit me?" *Lord, let me get out of here before Gandhi and this cracker get me in trouble!* "I'm just getting some ice for my drink," he said, as he opened the fridge.

Simmonds unclenched his jaw and let his hands fall to his sides. Gandhi was staring at him over the top of his glasses, and Skippy was flaring his nostrils.

Gorillas about to attack! Oh yeah, and SGT Wickett on CQ, I'll be the one getting the blame when he writes his report. Thanks again, SGT Preston, you know how they all stick together! They'll all say I started some racial crap and the next thang you know, I'll get busted and they'll take money out of my pay. Command always believes Blacks over white people. We don't have any rights, anymore! "Tell y'all what, I'm going back downstairs. Just don't mess with Eiric's stuff." *Or mine!* Simmonds left the room and Skippy threw a piece of ice at the door when it closed. Simmonds flipped both middle fingers at the closed door. *I hate black people!*

"Gandhi, I wish he would have said something, I would have been on him like white on rice!" Skippy shouted. Inside his head, another track played. *That was close! If Big Greasy had hit him, he would have killed that sucker! Then, they would have locked his black ass up and thrown away the key. Even with a room full of witnesses. Yeah, right, three black people against one, poor defenseless white guy? That's an open and shut case. They would find a way to get all of us, even E, and he wasn't even in the room!*

Skippy reflexively ducked as Greasy swung a slow haymaker in his direction. "Yeah, right!" Greasy laughed. "I'm sure Simmonds was worried to death about your malnourished ass attacking him!"

Gandhi sat on the edge of Eiric's bed with one thought in his head. *I hate white people.*

Eiric was still on the phone when Simmonds walked past on his way to the TV room. *Call my name so I can have an excuse to hang up,* he thought as he tried to get Simmonds' attention, but Simmonds didn't see him.

Screw you and your Bros! I'm not helping you! She was good enough for you to have sex with so she should be good enough to talk to. That's what she gets. When you lay down with trash, you wake up with trash. Then, you get treated like trash. Maybe next time you'll stick with your own kind. That is, if any self respectin' white man would have you! I know I wouldn't! Once you go Black, I ain't touchin' that!

Simmonds laughed to himself as he rejoined the crowd still watching the movie. He could tell from their faces upon seeing his return that they were still upset he had ruined the movie for them earlier. He didn't care.

Screw y'all too, Gorillas! Where are we? Oh, yeah, Sarge is going home to catch his cheatin' wife in the act. They're gonna hate me for this but, screw 'em! "Man, this is my favorite part!" he yelled. "Go Sarge, climb up to the roof, swing down through the window and rip off his Johnson, then, shoot her right between the eyes!" The men in the room cursed at Simmonds, as most of them began to file out of the TV room, not waiting to see his prediction come true. He laughed to himself. *Screw all you niggers!*

At the desk, Eiric was finishing his conversation. Gabe had just told him she loved him, to which he replied, "Me too," and hung up. He went back to his room and found his buddies still fuming over Simmonds. Gandhi and Skippy were coughing and Big Greasy was squatting with his back to Simmonds' pillow.

There was a foul odor drifting to meet Eiric at the door. He waved his hand in front of his face, thinking, *what's going on in here? No, tell me he didn't!* He yelled as he closed the door, "Hey, what are you doing? Get away from his stuff! I don't play that! Respect his stuff like you respect mine! Why do we always hang out in my room, anyway?"

"'Cause your room is bigger and you said we could come anytime," offered Skippy, as the three of them returned to his side of the room.

"Yeah, okay! But I told you to stay on my side. What are you doing in Simmonds' area?"

"Because he called Gandhi a 'nigger,'" said Greasy.

"He did what?" asked Eiric.

"Called him a 'Black nigger,' then he tried to hit me, but I dusted the floor with his raggedy ass!" Greasy continued.

"So that's why he ignored me downstairs," Eiric reflected.

Skippy spoke up. "He didn't call anybody a 'nigger,' but he wanted to. It was all over his face. Gandhi was messing with his head, then, all of a sudden, he broke down like he was gonna hit my boy, Greasy, just because he stood up to get some ice!"

"What?" Eiric asked. "He was gonna hit Greasy because he wanted some ice?"

"Yeah, Man! You shoulda been here! He jumped up, he had the eye of the tiger, and he was like, 'Wuuu-ahhh!' up in here!" Skippy balanced on one leg, with his hands in the air, in a shaky, Kung Fu crane-style.

Gandhi threw a pillow at him. "Man, sit down! You look like a scarecrow! They exaggerated a little, E. But it was getting tense in here. I know that redneck hates me. Correction, hates us."

"So, what? You don't like him, or them," answered Eiric. He picked his pillow up off the floor and sat on his bed. Gandhi got up and walked to the middle of the room.

"It's not about liking anybody," he began, "or disliking them. He's never done anything to me and as far as I know, I've never done anything to him. But I know that anytime he looks at me, or anybody that's darker than he is, he's looking down his nose at us. That uneducated, backwoods, yuk-mouth, inbred, redneck has the nerve to look down at anybody? Negro, please!"

"I've never seen you look lovingly at anybody white," Eiric quipped.

"You also don't see any crap like this," he said, pointing at a Confederate flag hanging on Simmonds' wall, "in my room! How do you put up with that?"

"It's an album cover and it's also called freedom of speech."

"Oh, freedom of speech? Well, let's look under his bed. I'm sure we'll find a whole lot of good stuff. Like a Klan hood and robe! And I know he would never leave home without a rope, just in case he wanted to unite a nigger with a tree limb. I don't have a problem with white people. I do have a problem with people that believe in Dash Americans."

"What?" asked Eiric, with a puzzled look.

"Uh-oh, here he goes," said Skippy. "Preach! Brother, father, reverend, Martin, Malcolm, triple X, almight-tee!" intoned Big Greasy with a hearty laugh.

Gandhi smiled before he continued. "You heard me. I said I have an issue concerning **Dash** Americans. You see, white people," he corrected himself as Eiric raised an eyebrow at him. "**Some** white people believe that they are Americans. Americans, that's it. Everybody that's not white gets a nice little label in front of a dash. Asian **Dash** American, Italian **Dash** American, Mexican **Dash** American, Black, Afro, or African **Dash** American, or whatever the fuck they want to call us! It doesn't matter, we're all **Dash** Americans, meaning we're less than they are. In math, what sign is used to subtract one thing from another? That's right, a little dash. Just like in math, that dash diminishes your status as an American. Oh yeah, that dash also takes something away from whatever ethnic term is in front of it. It's watered down.

"It's just like mixing colors. Like when you add white to black. You get grey. Or, add white to red, you get pink. Consider Private Hassan and Specialist Akbar. I hang out a lot with both of them. They're some cool Brothers. Hassan was born in Tehran but his family moved to the States when he was little. Akbar lived in Texas all his life, was born there, but his parents are from Iran. Akbar outranks Hassan but those rednecks in his platoon, like SGT Preston, give him shit details but they won't fuck with Hassan. They give him all kinds of respect because they think he's from an oil family or maybe a terrorist group. I've heard them saying that and I know you guys have, too. Now, with Akbar, they give him hell. They mock his accent...it's the same as Hassan's...make fun of his 'Ko-Ran,' and they crack jokes about his family working at a gas station. Think about it. Akbar is a joke because he's Iranian **Dash** American, but Hassan is feared and respected because he's an Iranian that moved to America. Akbar laughs that shit off because he grew up hearing that, but Hassan gives them the stone-face.

"If I say 'Mexican,' you think of somebody like SGT Ortiz, proud, hard-working, brave, man's man. Somebody you want by your side in a fight or just to hang out with. He's smart as hell, too. He taught himself to speak English by watching *Sesame Street* when he joined the Army. Now if I say 'Mexican-American,' you think about somebody sneaking across the border, an illegal alien, as 'they' say, mowing lawns, afraid of being deported. Same thing goes for us. If I say 'African,' you think about kings and queens, Zulu warriors, cradle of civilization, pyramids, but if I say 'African-American,' all you see is Tyrone and La-Treeka walking around with their pants pulled down, shoplifting, smoking weed, on welfare, or headed to jail."

He paused for effect, with his index finger pressed to his lips. "Now, if I say 'American,' you think of what? Blond hair, blue eyes, no lips or hips, but good credit-having, police-loving, PTA meeting-attending individuals, with country club memberships and dogs named 'Rover!' Rover lives inside the house, and eats real dog food, not table scraps." Everybody laughed at this. At some point, each one's family had owned a dog that ate whatever the family ate or lived out their lives chained to a tree or a stake in the ground, knowing freedom only when a collar broke or a chain needed to be untangled.

"Man, let's get outta here," Greasy said to Skippy. "This is gettin' too deep for me. Let's go find some food."

"Damn skippy. Easy E, are you coming or are you gonna let the Great Gandhi finish his sermon?"

"Y'all go ahead, I'm not hungry," Eiric replied.

"Alright, Gandhi, Easy E, be cool!" said Big Greasy as he and Skippy gave Eiric and Gandhi their secret handshake. When they finished dapping, they all yelled, "Horsemen...Forever!" then Skippy and Greasy left the room.

Gandhi settled down on the chair that Skippy had left behind while Eiric poured a touch of cognac into his glass of soda. He didn't like to drink, but, every once in a while, he liked the taste of this combination, lots of cola with a trace of yak. He broke the silence left behind from the departure of his two other friends.

"Man, I'm gonna miss those knuckleheads! Anyway, Gandhi, you really believe all that stuff you were saying? Where did you read that?" He sipped from his glass.

"I didn't read it anywhere, Bruh. I observe things around me and I make up my own mind about what I see and hear and feel. So, yes, I do believe in what I say. Nobody else has to believe it, but I wish some people did." He was staring straight at Eiric.

Eiric caught his hint. They didn't always see eye to eye but Gandhi was his best friend. What he thought was important to Eiric. He especially wondered what he really thought about him, since they were so different.

Gandhi was from New York, Eiric was from a small town in North Carolina, Murfsburg. Gandhi could take down shot after shot of tequila without any effect but Eiric's cognac and coke, heavy on the cola and weaker than a virgin pina colada, made his chest burn with each swallow. Eiric was easy going, quiet, friendly. Gandhi was always ready to do battle with words, starting or entering an argument with anyone over any insult, real or imagined.

Eiric shrugged his shoulders then nodded at his friend. "Man, I hear what you're saying, and I kinda understand what you were saying, this time. But, Man... 'Dash Americans?' You've got too much time on your hands, sitting around thinking of things like that. You need to go out and get some!"

"I go out more than enough. I'm just not into white girls. I don't have anything in common with them. I can't share myself fully with them because I might offend them. The few Sisters over here act like their stuff is made out of gold. They make you jump through hoops just to 'allow' you to buy them a drink. And I'm talking about the ugly ones. The really attractive Sisters only want Americans, you know, Chad and Lance. I guess that's payback because Brothers go crazy for all these German girls that are so easy to scoop up."

"Don't forget about my favorite, Turkish! Then there's Greek, Italian, French, Romanian, Russian, and your favorite, War Babies!"

"I didn't forget. To me, if they're here in Germany, they're German. Just like back home, they would be American. But, I do like War Babies because when I see them, I see my favorite color...black!"

"You do know black is not a color, don't you?"

"Who says it's not a color?"

"Everyone knows it's not a color. It's the absence of all color. Look it up in the dictionary."

"So, what color are these boots?"

"Black. Well, we call them 'black,' but really our eyes can't make out a color, so we just see a negative image. It's scientific."

"Oh, you mean 'science' tells you these black boots have no color and you believe that? Hmm, that's interesting. White scientists tell you that black is not even a color and you believe it without question? We both see these black boots in front of us, but they say we really don't see the color 'black' because black is the absence of all color?"

"That's right, we don't see a color. At best, we see a shade."

"So what color is air?" Eiric just stared blankly at his friend. "Air is clear. It seems to me that 'clear' is the absence of all color." Gandhi smiled as he returned to his previous conversation about bi-racial women.

"Anyway, War Babies are pretty, and they are black, but they're angry because they're mixed. For the most part, they hate us worse than some white people do, because their fathers treated their mothers like dirt before leaving them knocked up when they bounced back to the States. Uh, speaking of which, what's up with Gabe?"

Eiric took a larger gulp of his drink. "Well, she won't be having a War Baby, that's for sure. It was killing me, but I stayed away from her the past couple of months. I had to pull out my alter ego, 'Jason Kennedy,' so I could get some play from other chicks. I knew the closer I got to leaving, the harder it would be to say bye to her, but she knows when I'm going home. She always knows when I'm at my parents' house. You know, when I went home on leave, I was always on the move, but she only called the house when I was there, like she was psychic."

"If you didn't want her to call, why did you give her their phone number?"

"Man, she told me something one night I'll never forget. She told me that her daddy found out about me. Now, her mom has known about me almost from the beginning, but she tried to hide it from him because he's very orthodox, and only wants her to be with another Turkish dude. So, when he found out she was in love with a black man, he tripped out. He didn't hit her or anything, but he told her she should be ashamed for loving me. I was about to get mad at him for saying some bull like that but she looked me in the eyes and I saw the water in hers. Then she said these words to me with that beautiful accent. 'He told me I should be ashamed, but with you, I have no shame.' Man, I never heard anything like that before."

"Aww, ain't that sweet!" Gandhi gushed.

"Fuck you! Man." *Why did I tell him that?* "I was going on leave so I had to give her the number after she said that. It got expensive, because we talked almost every day while I was home. I didn't care about the bill because she always sounds so good. She also called a lot and kept in touch with my mom while I was over in the desert." *Mama really likes her because she could tell Gabe loves me.* "I told her at the start, when we first started kicking it, not to fall in love with me!"

"But you love her, too, Man."

"That's funny. You don't like white people, refuse to date anybody that's not at least half-black, but you're pushing me to be with a white woman."

"She's Turkish, not White," Gandhi corrected. *There's a difference.*

"You're right. You encourage me to get with a **Turkish** woman, even though you never would. Me, I don't care what skin she wears as long as she treats me right. I'll date anybody—but I can't marry anybody that's not black."

"Marry?"

"Yeah, she, I mean, we have talked about it before." Gandhi smiled at him before Eiric yelled, "Alright, I love the girl! I just can't marry her. If I marry her, that means I might have to stay here. I don't want to live in Germany, and I don't want to stay in the Army all my life. Mixed couples are normal in the military, but I don't want this life, I want to go to school. There's no way I could take her home. If I take her to

Murfsburg, somebody's gonna say something stupid that's gonna make me say or do something stupid. I don't want to expose her to that kind of crap.

"Over here, it's cool. We go out and it feels normal, no stares, no name-calling. Back home it would be different. I don't want to live under a microscope, worried about what other people are thinking and waiting for some racial powder keg to explode. Plus, she might even get a mind to call me something, and then what? I also think about our kids and the pressure they would have from stupid people around us. Naw, I can't do it. That's why I only dated white girls over here because I didn't want to fall in love."

Wow, that made no damn sense. "But you did!" Gandhi reminded him. "I'm not a racist, I'm a realist. People have distinct perspectives of this world, and a lot of them come from racial views. I think you two should be together, not because she's white and you need to prove something, but because you both love each other. You started something with her, something I couldn't do. Now, you need to make a decision you can live with and be proud of. Forget other people."

"The decision has already been made. I'm going home, alone. I'll love her forever, especially for her letters during the war, but I can't give any more than that."

"Alright, E. So, what's her name?"

"Gabe." He was starting to get a bit annoyed with Gandhi. *Why are you so concerned about this? I'm trying to get her out of my head.*

"Not Gabe, your lady back home."

"Don't know, I haven't met her yet."

"You're a brave man, giving up a sure thing to chase a dream," Gandhi said.

"I'm not chasing anything. When the time is right, it'll happen. Besides, you're the brave one."

"What do you mean?" asked Gandhi as he took another drink.

"I mean, the way you always speak out about everything. It's like you're trying to bring back the 60's and start your own movement, or something."

Eiric was smiling but Gandhi looked him in the eye and spoke with a somber expression. "Somebody has to say something. Too many people stand around being quiet, ignoring things happening all around them." Gandhi's gaze seemed to burn right through Eiric's soul.

Eiric often wondered what people really thought about him and nobody's opinion mattered more than his friend staring at him. *I suppose you mean me?* "So, what you're saying is, it's okay to be a champion for every cause? Make some noise, create some waves and you'll make some kind of progress? I don't think so. You speak out all the time about what's not right around here, but I don't see anybody changing anything. Oh, I forgot. They do make **some** changes...they've made it impossible for you to get promoted."

"My mouth hasn't prevented me from getting promoted. It's kept me from being advanced ahead of less deserving suck-ups. I'm never going to kiss anybody's butt to get ahead, but you know what? After I've spent enough time doing my job in my current rank, and I've **earned** enough points, they'll have to promote me. No ass kissing required. I'm not concerned about that, though. I care about letting people know when something is not right. I do try to pick my battles, but I can't stand by quietly while somebody's rights as a human being are being violated. You should be uncomfortable if, knowing me the way you do, somebody in power, some white person, opened a door for you because you smiled at him but slammed it in my face because I refused to show him all my teeth."

Oh, so I'm a grinning and shuffling Uncle Tom? Eiric thought. His face must have reflected this thought because Gandhi's face softened and his intuition, something Eiric admired and envied, kicked in.

"Look, Man, I'm not trying to call you some tap-dancing-house-Negro that, 'Lub him sum dem dare white folk!' E, you're one of the most intelligent people I've ever met and you're the best friend I ever had."

Eiric's head snapped back as those unexpected words hit him. *Whoa! All this time I thought you only liked me 'cause I was the only one that actually listens to your crazy speeches. So, I'm not just some country bumpkin! I'm your best friend! I've always considered you to be my best friend, but I never knew I was your best friend.*

Eiric kept thinking about his status as best friend while Gandhi continued to speak. "I don't expect you to be like me. I don't want you to be like me. I respect you for being color blind, and I wish I could be more like that." Again, Eiric's head went back as his ego accepted another high-five. "I've tried, but I can't. I can't hold my tongue when I feel something is wrong."

"You do keep things stirred up," Eiric agreed.

"Somebody has to! Look, if you see somebody killing another person and you do nothing, you don't try to stop him, you don't try to save the person, you don't call the cops, you don't provide a witness or help convict him in court, then, you're just as guilty of murder. I don't believe all white people are bad or prejudiced. I don't believe all black people are good or unbiased. I do believe that Blacks and

Whites live in two different worlds on the same planet. How is it, a white cop can give a white man a ticket for a traffic violation, but beat down a law abiding, **unarmed**, Brother for the same thing? We see it and say it's foul, yet white people look at the same picture and say the police are doing the right thing? 'The black guy probably did something to provoke it or he already has a criminal record, so he deserves it!' In that case, do we even need judges, lawyers, or jurors, since the cops are doing their jobs?"

"I don't know," Eiric answered truthfully. "Why do you see everything in black and white, where white people are always doing something to us? I'm sure you know at least one black person that did something wrong to a white person for no reason at all."

"I don't see everything in black and white. I could compare any race against another, but since I'm black, and there are so many good examples to back me up, I choose to talk about my exact opposite. Let me tell you a true story. When I was growing up, I was one of three Blacks in all my classes. We were called, 'Special,' because we made good grades in advanced subjects.

"I didn't mind being in classes with mostly white kids, at first. I thought I was cool with them because I had the best grades in the class and they called me, 'Professor Portland.' I tried to fit in, to be friends with them, but every chance they got, they let me know I was just another nigger to them. My full nickname was, 'That Nigga, Professor Portland!' So, after a while, I started slacking off because I wanted to be back with the black kids. You know what? They treated me worse than the white kids did. They used to call me, 'Oreo,' because I didn't 'talk Black.' I was forced to be in class with white people that didn't want me there and when I tried to hang out with the Brothers, I usually got my ass kicked for, 'trying to be White.' My Moms thought I was in a gang because I always came home all busted up." He shook his head at this memory.

"Before I joined the Army, I knew these Brothers, Marcus, Tyrone, and Shemar. Everybody called them Ty-D, Mark-Mark, and Vicious. They were thugs, and they used to do thug shit. One day, there was a story in the news about a European tourist, a white guy, who had been mugged near our projects and was in serious condition in the hospital. Nobody knew the guy. No one came to the hospital to check on him, so people were urged to come forward if they had any information. He hadn't done a thing to anybody, just came to the States to see the sites in New York.

"Anyway, these Brothers were bragging about how they had come across some funny-talking white guy who was flashing his cash and asking for directions. They gave him directions...to an alley where they robbed him and left him for dead. They thought it was hilarious. Everybody in the neighborhood thought it was funny, you know, like it served him right. He shouldn't have been there in the first place, checking out the hood like it was a zoo."

Gandhi swallowed hard before going on. "Anyway, they kept spending his money and living large until the cops rolled up on them. Ty-D still had the man's wallet and the others had deutsche marks in their pockets. Ty-D and Mark-Mark went to prison, but the cops blasted Vicious. They said they thought he was reaching for a gun, but no weapon was found." He looked Eiric in the eyes. "I dropped a dime on them, but I can't tell anybody because that would get me killed. I couldn't even use the reward money because everyone would have figured out it was me. I sent the money, anonymously, to pay for Dude's hospital bill."

"What you did was cool, Gandhi," Eiric said, very impressed that his friend had risked his life for a stranger. "But you see what I mean. Black people did something bad to a white person, not the other way around."

Gandhi nodded. "Yeah. A week after I turned in those Brothers, I was still feeling pretty good about myself. I mean, I hated sending those guys to jail, and getting

Shemar killed, but what they did was wrong. I was walking to my grandma's apartment. I had picked up some groceries for her from the market. I saw some kids nearby playing ball just, all of a sudden, take off running. I knew something was going down, so I looked around and saw this cop car rolling up on me. I hadn't done anything wrong so I didn't run. They were looking my way when they got out so I looked around to see who they were after. They were coming for me!

"In my mind, I was like, 'They're not after me, I helped them catch the bad guys!' But they didn't know that. They just saw a target, a guy walking while black! Man, one of them grabbed me and threw me up against this fence beside the walkway. Then he slammed my face down on the hood of the car. My nose was bleeding, my face was scraped up, plus my wrist, arm, and shoulder felt like he broke them." He paused before going on with his story.

"I never felt so much pain like what I felt that day with my arm jacked up behind my back. I started screaming, 'Officer, I didn't do anything!' The one that wasn't holding me said, 'I know! This is so you **won't** do anything!' I was trying hard not to cry but it hurt so bad. I was like, 'This is not right, Officers, I didn't do anything! I bought this for my grandma!'

"Then the one holding me punched me in the kidney and threw me on the ground. He said, 'It's a Black thing! You wouldn't understand.' I watched those two crackers get in their car laughing at me. The one who threw me the beating pointed his finger at me and curled his finger, you know, pulling the trigger at me. I stopped crying but I was shaking so bad because I felt so helpless. To them, I was just another low-life, innocent, until proven black!

"My grandma's eggs, Man, they were crushed. I didn't have any more money because I didn't keep any of the reward, so I couldn't replace them. Of course, when I got to her place, I got in trouble for breaking her eggs and getting them all over the rest of the groceries. When my Moms got home, she went off on me. She threatened to put me out since I wanted to be a thug so bad. I tried to tell her what really happened but she wouldn't even listen. If I hadn't already joined the Army, she would have put me out on the street that day. People saw what happened but they didn't tell my Moms nothing! Black or white, if somebody sees something wrong, they have to speak up."

"There you go again, black against white."

"All right! So, I used black and white! Face it, nobody else is against us the way Whites are! No other race is against any other race the way white people are. You know why?"

"Naw, but I'm sure you do." Eiric was shaking his head.

Gandhi looked at his friend then lowered his head as he allowed a sneaky smile to take over his face. "The reason why white people hate every other race on this planet is because...they are not from this planet!" Eiric covered his eyes with his right hand and groaned.

"Hold on, Dog, listen! I believe white people are aliens from outer space! It's the only explanation that makes sense for a lot of things. Skinny lips, flat butts, sun burns! Every other culture has their beliefs grounded in nature, you know, herbal remedies, clothes from animal skins, and even animal-like spirits that control weather, fate, and other things they couldn't explain. And, other races believe in a Supreme Being, God, Buddha, Allah, whatever. White people believe in **science**. Other cultures made due with what nature provided, living in caves, grass huts, tepees, even igloos. White people came along and leveled forests to build houses.

"We see a storm and accept it as God's will, where they have to investigate, study, forecast, and try to control it. Tornado chasers? Cloud-seeding to make rain or change the course of hurricanes? Who thinks of this kind of stuff? I mean, who thought about breaking down atoms and redesigning genes? Huh? Who came up with the idea for cloning and artificial sweeteners? White people! Who's making telescopes and rockets and deep space probes? White people! They're aliens, trying to get back where they came from.

"You see, a long time ago, there were these cool white aliens who found themselves stuck with this group of messed up white aliens. The cool ones started flying around looking for a place to drop their bad asses off! They couldn't just beam them out into the vacuum of space, so they kept looking until they found Earth. They said, 'Hey, that looks like a good spot!' dropped them off in Europe and hit the light-speed button! See ya!"

"Wouldn't want to be ya!" Eiric laughed.

"Exactly!" Gandhi was also laughing. "Now you know why white people have tried to wipe out all the other races since they got here! They took out the cavemen first and said, 'Man, this is gonna be easier than we thought! Earthlings are punks!' But they didn't kill off everybody, at first. They were outnumbered, but because they saw we were compatible, they bred with humans, increasing their numbers. Of course, with each new generation, a lot of their alien culture and knowledge was diluted. It's important to realize, the original aliens who were left behind were not the cream of the crop, elite aliens. These were the regular-Joe, low-life aliens, but they were still more advanced than humans. When they were dropped off, they were left empty-handed. No gadgets, and no lasers meant they had to start from scratch.

"Come on, cross-bows and catapults were just normal products of evolution? Airplanes, spaceships, cars, guns, atomic bombs...all because these aliens have been trying to get back home or get rid of the rest of us! Who do you think those other people were in the Bible when Cain killed Able? Adam and Eve were their parents, created by God, so where did those people come from that Cain went out to live with? Alien white people! These aliens almost wiped out the Indians, I mean, Native **Dash** Americans. Enslaved Jews and Blacks and killed us by the thousands. Stole from the Mexicans and killed them for trying to keep what was theirs. The Holocaust. And everybody's favorite, the bombs they used

to destroy the Japanese! Notice they didn't
drop nukes in blue-eyed, blond-haired
Germany.   I tell you, they're nothing but
Earth pillaging, race-raping, alien Vikings!"

The two men laughed for a while, each
picturing a different version of little green
men with horned helmets and bloody
swords doing vile things to the planet. Eiric
was the first to speak when they regained
their composure.

"Aliens? White people are aliens? Man,
you're crazy!"

"Yes, yes, yes, thank you very much! Oh,
Man, I forgot about this. Elvis has been
dead 200 years and they still see him
everywhere! Alien encounters!" They
laughed for a few minutes, coughing and
gasping for air.

"Seriously, E, let me ask you a question.
You're from the South, right?" Eiric
nodded, knowing his friend already knew
where he was from. "Then explain
something to me. Why does every town in
the South have a park, or a bridge, or a
street dedicated to some Confederate
soldier?"

Eiric shifted uncomfortably as he shrugged his shoulders. "I don't know what you're talking about."

Gandhi continued unfazed by his friend's answer. "When I was stationed in Georgia, I rode through a lot of towns with my boys after duty. We went to Florida, South Carolina, and a little bit in your home state, and one thing kept bugging me. Everywhere we went, I saw Confederate this and rebel that. Statues, parks, shopping malls, flags, plaques, Man, you name it. Constant reminders that these people wanted to keep us slaves so bad that they went to war. And everywhere I went, there were black people just going on about their business, content with having a rebel flag over their heads."

"I'm not an expert on the subject, but I think you saw that stuff because it's part of history. It's just a way to honor the dead."

"So, you're saying it's all meant to pay tribute to the brave soldiers who died in the Civil War?"

"Yep! Nothing sinister about it, it's just about history and brave soldiers." Eiric was pleased at his answer, because he thought he had stopped Gandhi in his tracks. Wrong.

"So where are all the monuments to remember the brave soldiers that fought for the North? Or for that matter, where are the monuments to honor all the brave slaves who died helping to make America's history?" Eiric sat there blinking, struggling to find an answer.

"It's not a matter of honor, Eiric, it's all about intimidation. Those memorials are just a means to thumb their noses at the Yankees, a way to confirm that the South will rise again. 'The South will rise again'...what does that mean? Did it mean the South would bounce back from a major set-back or does it mean someday they'll be fighting again to enslave minorities?

"Listen, any person of color growing up around these tributes to the Confederacy has to feel something when they pass them by. You think pride is what they feel? No. Maybe they feel a sense of longing for the past? I don't think so. I think they feel shame, ashamed to see a constant reminder that our people used to be property. I think they feel powerless, hopeless, because they know there's nothing they can do about it. I think they feel afraid. Somewhere in their minds, they're afraid it could happen again."

Gandhi paused to allow this to sink in. "How long have you been in Germany?"

"Not including Desert Storm, three years."

"That's a long time. I bet you've been all over, right?" Eiric nodded and Gandhi continued. "Me too. Tell me something. Have you ever seen any Nazi statues? How about any parks named after Hitler or any of his generals?" Eiric just stared at him.

"No, you haven't. And you haven't seen any swastikas flying on government buildings or plastered on people's cars. You know why you don't see any tributes to the Third Reich? Because even though those were brave soldiers and what they did is part of Germany's history, the bottom line is...the Nazis were wrong. Dead wrong. Nobody's celebrating or paying tribute to the Nazis, except maybe some skinheads.

Eiric, our country, the 'Home of the Free,' builds bridges and keeps up statues to honor slave owners and the soldiers that fought to keep us in chains."

"Well, not where I'm from," Eiric said flatly.

"Then I take back what I said about all Southern cities allowing that crap. It's good to know that there are some places down there that are not filled with rednecks and complacent Negroes that allow that bull. One day, I've gotta come check you out. Look at you, Man. You're on your way back to the crib! What's the first thing you gonna do when you get home?"

Now here was a question Eiric could answer with ease. "I'm gonna get some real food!" He was happy the conversation had changed.

"I heard that! There's nothing like a good meal from your Moms!"

"Yeah, Man. I can't wait to taste Mama's fried chicken, corn bread and pecan pie!"

Gandhi laughed, "Well, I don't know about that, but I'll take your word that it's good. Eiric, you're lucky, no more chow halls, no more field duty, and no more living with people you don't like or don't know. I wish I was short, too!"

"Gandhi, do me a favor. Lay off Simmonds when I leave."

"Why?" Gandhi asked with a grin.

"I made friends with this dude, so I'm asking you, as my friend, to leave the boy alone."

"I'll do it for you but I gotta know why. I mean, he's a grown man and I think he can handle himself." *Come on, spill the beans, what's that cracker been saying about me? I know, he wants to hit me but he's afraid of what you might say.*

"I'm only telling you this so you'll understand, not so you can use this against him. You can't tell anybody what I'm about to tell you." Eiric waited until Gandhi gave his word.

"I promise, I won't tell a soul...Brother!" Eiric shook his head and Gandhi laughed, "Alright, alright, I won't say a word to anybody. Word is bond! Now, what's up?"

"Man, he's scared of you." Gandhi smiled as those words echoed in his head.

Eiric quickly tried to clarify as he realized that was the wrong thing to say to the wrong person. "Wait a minute, it's not like that. He's not scared of 'you,' he's afraid of 'us.' Black people. We were in here talking one night and he just came out and told me something I couldn't believe. He told me that before he joined the Army, he had never seen a black person." Gandhi's smile disappeared and his eyes grew larger. "Yep. He said he had never seen a real, live black guy, except on TV and in movies. He always thought that was just make-up. When he got to Basic Training and saw all those Brothers with real dark skin, he said he didn't know how to act. He was freaked out."

"Come on, Man. E, he **never** saw a black person?"

"He said there were no minorities at all where he was from. He had seen some Mexicans before, but never any black people. That's when he started thinking that everything he saw on TV about us was true. Since Mexicans were real, we must be real, and if we existed, we must all be bangers, pimps, and thugs. He said he never even said the N word until he was in Basic. That was when he called home to tell his people that they were everywhere. Of course, his family already knew." Gandhi rolled his eyes and shook his head.

"Yeah, I know, he's not the sharpest tool in the shed, but he's really okay. He just doesn't know any better."

"So, why did he confess this to you?"

Eiric didn't want to tell him but he couldn't think of a good lie. "He told me because he was puzzled by me. He never saw a black man like me on TV. He thought they were all like..." Eiric let his statement trail off as he looked away.

"Like what?" Gandhi asked.

Eiric looked him in the eye and said, "Like you. Always confrontational, always...negative. Those are the images he's always seen. He was confused because he liked me, after he had to be my roomie. Sometimes, he even forgets that I'm black because I act like one of his buddies back home."

The new look on Gandhi's face told Eiric he had just said the wrong thing. That look of disgust didn't last long. "Okay, Eiric, I won't mess with Simmonds anymore and no one else will hear what you just told me, at least not from me. Now, you can promise me something. Promise me, that one day you'll be less concerned with appealing to white people and more concerned with being true to yourself. I know you want to remain color blind but don't be blind to the truths right in front of your eyes. Nobody can fault you for calling a spade a spade."

Eiric stood up, his posture, expression and voice fueled by anger. "I'm not trying to please white people, this is me! This is who I am! If I ain't black enough for you, you'll have to excuse me, that's how God made me!"

Gandhi looked up at his friend, who now looked more like an enemy. Gandhi's face was relaxed and he spoke these words in a calm, soothing voice. "Be cool, Eiric." There was no threat in what Gandhi said. He had not intended to upset Eiric so this was his way of offering an apology for going too far with his words. Eiric understood and Gandhi was relieved to watch the rage melt away from his friend. His best friend. Some would say, his only friend. "We cool?" Gandhi asked, meaning, "Sorry."

"Yeah, we're cool. I'm sorry about that, Man. I just don't like people saying stuff like that about me. I believe in the Bible, I believe in the Golden Rule. You know, do unto others? Even devils will like other devils. I'm not going to hate somebody just because they hate me, and I'm not about to start the revolution! I'm just me, Eiric Lesson, plain, old, country boy."

"Naw, Man!" Gandhi said as he got to his feet. He extended his hand and Eiric immediately shook it. "You're a positive black man. Brother, I'm gonna miss you." Gandhi headed for the door, as it was getting late and they both had to get up early for duty. He paused at the door a moment after opening it. "I'm gonna miss your brain. Nite, Eiric." He closed the door and Eiric heard him yell, "I'm still coming to Murfsburg, or whatever the hell you call it, to check you out!"

Eiric laughed in the empty room. His friends were gone and soon, he would be gone for good. He spoke, apparently to the door, "I'm gonna miss your brain too, Bruh." That night, like most others, sleep had no trouble finding Eiric. Although falling asleep was easy for him, he seldom had a restful night, thanks to an endless series of nightmares. He would wake up tired even after nine hours of sleep. Most people can tell you what they saw or heard in their dreams. Eiric never remembered his nightmares, a strange fact considering he didn't just witness his dreams he participated in them, talking, waving, running, and screaming as events unfolded.

Many nights, Simmonds was awakened by spine-chilling screams that forced him to seek refuge downstairs in the TV room. He was so frightened by Eiric's nocturnal adventures in hell that he often actually looked forward to CQ. Simmonds wasn't alone. He was often met by a small crowd of their neighbors gathered outside their door, wondering what the noise was all about. At first, he tried to cover up for

Eiric, telling the other soldiers that Eiric had received bad news from home. But, as the dreams continued, and the screaming intensified, Simmonds was forced to tell them the truth. After all, there are only so many favorite uncles that could have died unexpectedly.

Eiric never remembered what happened at night so he was always taken aback by the uneasy looks and comments like, "You ain't right!" he routinely received. This night would be different, as every detail of his last dream would remain vividly clear.

Eiric's first dream was a rerun. It was a long running horror show that had been playing, without his knowledge, for months since the events actually took place. It started out pleasant enough, with dazzling sunlight, lots of smiling faces, and soldiers clustered in small groups enjoying a holiday feast. There was a twenty-table chess tournament, with stacked up ammo cases as the tables, surrounded by soldiers with serious faces. Others chased soccer balls, and footballs, and spiked volleyballs in the sand.

The pleasantries didn't last long. Victory yells and dances were quickly replaced by explosions and bodies convulsing in pain. Rivers of blood flowed from huge, open wounds. Men stumbled in aimless circles, searching for their missing limbs. One of these men held up an amputated arm but dropped it back onto a growing stack of arms as the skin color did not match his own.

The wind began to blow and sand swirled into an impenetrable curtain obscuring the battlefield. When the cloak was lifted, the ground began to move. Five mounds grew from the dirt, rising like lumps on a cartoon character's head. From the top of each mound, a slender stalk burst through, spraying sand and blood in all directions. The branches swayed in the breeze, slowly at first, then increasing in velocity until they were almost a blur. More sand flew away to reveal the "roots" of the stalks. The stalks were not plants. They were tails, furiously wagging tails attached to snarling, snapping, skeletal dogs. Huge, jaundiced, red-rimmed eyeballs bulged atop muzzles filled with fangs that dripped chords of frothy, venomous saliva. The sputum sizzled as it hit the sand, releasing an acrid aroma of burnt oil, rubber, and flesh.

This pack of emaciated canines took off howling until they reached a darkened lump on the ground. It was the body of a fallen soldier. Eiric was unable to tell if the soldier was American or Iraqi as his face was buried in the sand. The nightmare hounds did not care which side the soldier had fought on. To them, he was now simply...food. They fiercely bit the air in defense of their staked-out portions. Like pistons, their heads plunged into the soft flesh, ripping off chunks of the man. Some of the pieces of meat were readily identified; arms and legs, while others appeared like taffy being pulled between the growling maws of the hungry dogs.

The contents of Eiric's stomach found their way to his mouth before splattering on the sand. He wanted to turn away from this scene but it held him in a trance. The picture of this grisly show became flooded with tears that refused to fall. This was no way for any soldier, any human being, to be treated. Eiric raised his rifle and fired blindly. There was no need to aim. In a dream, much like an action movie, the hero's bullets always find their marks. As each hound fell, the others in the pack turned on their fallen brother and continued feasting, oblivious to their own impending doom, until they all were heaped in a steaming, blood covered pile. As if by magic, Eiric was standing on top of this pile staring down at the half-eaten soldier. He could now see the man's face looking up at him. The face was his.

He clenched his eyes shut and shook his head to rid himself of this image. In his bed, copying the movements of his dream-self, Eiric shook his head and screamed. Eiric's cry was heard outside his room by a neighboring soldier returning from a bar. The other man eyed Eiric's door as he fumbled to unlock his own. As soon as the man entered his room he slammed the door behind him and turned the deadbolt. Inside

Eiric's room, the crying stopped but the dreaming continued.

After a few minutes of tossing in bed, Eiric settled into a comfortable position that relaxed his strained muscles. The high-pitched screams were downgraded to subdued snores. Behind his eyelids, his eyeballs began to move rapidly, causing new images to materialize. Instead of a sandy battlefield, Eiric found himself standing on black asphalt surrounded by store fronts. Overhead, a huge banner that read, "Welcome Home, Brave Soldier!" was suspended between the shops. Eiric turned around, and every direction he looked, the banner remained in sight, taunting him.

Familiar faces appeared, cheering for him. He saw his mother and father. His sister and brother, aunts, uncles, cousins, and family he barely knew. His pastor was there along with the whole church congregation, all in their Sunday best. Friends from his school and neighborhood all filled the street, forming a narrow corridor for Eiric to navigate. He moved slowly through the cheering mob. His body rocked as he received numerous pats on his shoulders. At the end of the aisle, a large, gray blur slowly began to come into focus.

A box, no, a pedestal rose from the ground. Emerging from the top of this granite edifice was a mighty war horse. His hind legs were firmly planted while his front legs pawed the air, frozen in time. Sitting in the saddle was a bearded Confederate general, brandishing a sword above his head that pointed south. For a moment, the horse and rider glared down at him with hateful sneers etched into their stone faces. Eiric tried but couldn't turn and run away.

Something, either the throng of well-wishers or the very ground itself, propelled him forward. He kept moving towards the statue until he splashed headfirst into a reflecting pool at its base. He resurfaced sputtering warm liquid as he looked up at the mounted soldier. The sword was now pointed directly at him. Eiric bobbed in the pool and his mouth filled again with the warm water. It was salty with a slight metallic taste. Wiping his forehead and mouth, he was stunned by the trail of red left on his wrist. It was not water. This was blood.

Franticly, he spun away from the statue to the crowd of his family and friends. They seemed to be waving to him from a distant shore. He tried to call to them but a forceful wave of blood smacked him in the face, choking away his breath and blurring his vision.

When his eyes cleared, he saw that even if he had been able to yell, nobody could have saved him. The happy faces that had greeted him only moments ago were now on fire. They still held onto their smiles and continued to applaud as their bodies melted and flowed into the scarlet reflecting pool. He was drowning in their blood. The likeness of the general and his horse danced on the ripples before him and he watched horrified as their sneers stretched into smiles. The waves then settled and he was able to read the inscription on the pedestal of this demonic monument. "We Will Rise Again!" The drowning man tilted his head back in a

useless attempt to remain afloat and
screamed from the depths of his lungs. A
searing rush of blood flooded his mouth,
completely choking off his yell of defiance.

In the barracks, soldiers all along the
long hallway were jostled from their sleep.
Some of them cursed. Some prayed. Others
simply shook their heads. A hollow voice,
like that of a tortured, disembodied spirit,
filled the deserted corridor. It seemed to
grow louder at each door it passed.

The sound was a single word, "Nooooo!"
drifting away in the dark, ripping through
the calm and leaving a wake of dread. In
one room, a lone soldier wiped his forehead
and mouth. He was soaked. The fluid on
his face was warm and salty. Eiric
stretched a trembling hand into the void
and found the switch to his desk lamp.
Harsh light filled the room forcing his
eyelids shut. Squinting, his eyes slowly
adjusted to the brightness. Eiric looked
down at his hand and then up to his mirror.
He was relieved to find his face and hand
covered only in sweat.

Several mornings later, Eiric again found that he was alone in his room, just staring at an empty wall. His side of the room was stripped bare. All of his personal belongings had already been shipped to the States, to his parents' home. He was wearing his dress green uniform, a requirement for his military flight, with only his two duffle bags and a carry-on for company. The other soldiers, his friends, were busy with their clean-up details after finishing a five-mile run. He could hear the commotion outside his door, and he easily put faces to voices as they passed by. He smiled then glanced at his watch. The smile faded as he realized it was time to leave. The van would be arriving to take him to his flight home. He gathered his bags and dropped a good-bye note on Simmonds' desk.

Outside the room, Eiric was greeted by friends who wished him good luck or wished that they were in his place. He made his way downstairs to turn in his room key to the CQ. The sergeant accepted the key and shook his hand. He then directed Eiric to drop his bags behind the desk. He explained that the van was still picking up others leaving for the States. As Eiric placed his bags on the floor, a familiar voice was heard cursing in the latrine. He and the CQ headed toward the restroom. Before they reached it, Gandhi charged out, still cursing and waving his hands.

"I give less than half a damn! Y'all can take my rank, take my money, my freedom, I don't care! I...am not...cleaning...that shit!" He looked at Eiric and his angry scowl turned into a smile. "What up, Bruh, ready for the World?"

Eiric returned his smile and nodded. "What's up with you? What's going on in there?"

"Man, S.O.S. after a payday weekend. Some nasty, sorry ass, **white** boy, with no home-training" Gandhi was yelling again, "wrote on the walls in the toilet stalls!"

"Come on, Dog, how do you know it was somebody white?" Eiric asked, as the CQ returned to his desk laughing.

"Because I don't know any Brothers that would," his voice rose again, "stick his hand in the toilet, grab a turd, and say, 'Hmmm, I think I'll use this since I forgot my pen.' Oh, and that's not all. Whoever did it, knew I had latrine duty, so they left me a message only a white person would. Plus, the asshole is still not used to indoor plumbing because they forgot to flush!"

"Oh, they forgot to flush?" Eiric laughed.

"You think it's funny? Come check this out." Gandhi led his friend into the restroom and made a quick left past the sinks, where other soldiers were cleaning, to the row of stalls in the back. A strong odor caused Eiric's nose to wrinkle. He cupped his hand over his nose and mouth as Gandhi opened the door of the last stall. "Look at this shit!"

Eiric stepped to the doorway, not really wanting to see floating logs, simply humoring his fried one last time. What he saw brought his breakfast to the back of his throat. Rising from the bowl of the toilet was a large, brown mound, resembling a volcano and decorated with a few tufts of toilet paper. He glanced unbelieving at his friend.

"Now I ask you, who else would keep shitting, not flushing, until it grew into this monster? And look at that," he directed, pointing to the message on the wall, scrawled in jagged, brown script. "Yeah clean my shit up—NIGGER!!!"

Eiric nodded his head and they made their way out of the restroom. When they entered the main hallway, he was startled as he found himself suddenly lifted to the ceiling.

"There you are, Bruh!" It was Big Greasy, holding him effortlessly over his head laughing. Greasy lowered him back to the ground and gave him a bear hug. "E, we thought you left without saying anything," he continued as he released his death grip.

"Damn skippy!" chimed Skip, as he punched Eiric in the shoulder.

"Man, y'all gone mess up my uniform and they won't let me fly home."

"Swim, Negro!" his three friends yelled back at him. They laughed and talked for a short while before the CQ called for Eiric. The van was out front. It was time for him to leave. Greasy and Skip picked up his duffle bags and Gandhi carried his smaller bag as they escorted Eiric to the waiting vehicle.

Two other men in dress greens were already inside and they stared out as the four men did some strange handshake and yelled something about, "Horsemen...Forever!" They laughed as they helped the driver pack his bags in the back of the van. Eiric then gave his friends a sober look.

"I'm really gonna miss you guys. If it hadn't been for y'all, I would've gone crazy. Crazier! I know we already said bye, but I have to say this before I leave. It's something we used to say in my church, called the Mizpah. 'The Lord watch between me and thee, when we are absent, one from the other.'" This was a verse often used at the close of a sermon at his small home church, so he was surprised that all three of his friends had joined in the recital, even adding, "There's no 'Amen,'" when it was finished. His face showed that he was impressed.

"We **have** been to church, Eiric!" Skip informed him.

Eiric put up his hands in surrender then took his seat in the van. He waved back at his friends as the van pulled off. He didn't look back, couldn't, thanks to the cramped compartment and stiff confines of his dress uniform. The other passengers sat in silence, full of understanding since, earlier, they had each said their own farewells to their buddies. Even with less crowding, none of the occupants dared look back at the friends they left behind.

As Eiric sat rigidly facing the front windshield, he felt a crushing sense of loneliness and his eyes began to moisten. With some effort, he turned his head to look out the window. He jumped at his reflection on the glass. His dark green uniform, with dazzling brass buttons, was fresh from the cleaners. A black tie was perfectly nestled, not too tight, not too loose, against a pressed pale green shirt. Neat rows of multi-colored ribbons lined up in formation beneath a shiny, silver medal. His suit was not the problem.

He was a well-dressed gargoyle with sagging shoulders, no chest, red, glistening eyes, dark, deep frown lines, and dry, pouting lips. The worn-out expression clashed with his crisp military wear. Focusing on the medal, he clenched his jaws and thought, *man up! I can't sit here, looking like a crybaby! I'm a soldier, a Combat Medic!* He inhaled noisily and, instantly, his shoulders lifted as his chest expanded. The frown lines disappeared, and his mouth retracted to its normal position. He darted his tongue out to moisten his lips and his eyes, now white, dried up. Funny thing about those dress green uniforms; they restrict full range of movement and they also excel at preventing tears from falling.

Back in the World

On a bad day, the drive from Ft Bragg to Murfsburg was about two and a half hours. Today must be a day from Hell. Over thirteen hours ago, Eiric boarded this bus in Ft Bragg and set out for Greensboro, where he would connect with another bus for the last leg to Murfsburg. On a bad day, Greensboro was only a half hour drive from home. Eiric was crumpled in his seat with his forehead pressed against the frigid window, staring blankly at the passing pine trees. Almost every part of his body hurt. The only area free of pain was his rear end, which had gone numb several hours ago. As each hour passed, Eiric recounted each milestone of his marathon journey home. This was his thirteenth calculation.

I don't believe this is happening. This is unreal. No, this is torture. I got up at five o'clock yesterday morning and put on this monkey suit. He was still wearing his dress uniform which still looked impressive after almost two days of wear.

I left Augsburg at seven-forty and got to Frankfurt at nine forty-five. My flight didn't leave until two pm. The flight took nine and half hours from Germany to New York. Only nine and a half hours to get from one country to another. Okay, so that's eleven thirty, in New York, twenty minutes on the ground for fuel, then back in the air for a two-hour flight to North Carolina. We hit the ground at one forty-five in the morning. At exactly zero two twenty, this damn bus headed out from Ft Bragg on the way to Greensboro. It's three pm, correction, fifteen hundred, and we just hit the city limits for the Boro. If the next bus to Murfsburg is not sitting at the station ready to roll out when we get there, I'm walking home.

Naw, the next bus has to be there. They wouldn't keep torturing me like this. We've already stopped at every town, every truck stop, every stop-sign in the state, so they would never think about making me wait any longer to get home. To get out of this uniform! I don't mind being in uniform on or near base, but away from the military, these

greens attract too much attention.
Unwanted attention, he thought.

As the bus rumbled through the streets of Greensboro on its way to the bus station, Eiric thought about the people who had taken an interest in his uniform during his trip. He was right about his attire being the focus of attention.

At first, just outside the base, no one really noticed. There were other uniformed military on the bus and too many walking and driving by for the locals to be awed. But, as they travelled farther away from the GI town and the bus emptied of the other soldiers, Eiric found himself the star of the show, as all eyes made a pilgrimage to his uniform and its colorful ribbons and shiny medals.

Indeed, the left breast of his jacket was heavy with the decorative record of his achievements in the Army. When curious civilians approached him with questions about his awards, he provided brief, humble explanations of each award and then smiled politely as they pretended to understand or care. Most of the admirers simply wondered how he had so many for such a young man.

In fact, for a regular, non-special ops soldier, Eiric had a display of ribbons that rivaled senior enlisted soldiers' and those of wizened generals. To the trained eye of a military member, past or present, Eiric's uniform told an impressive story. It told them he had done a lot in just a short time, just three years, according to his service stripe. Some measured his success by the number of ribbons, stacked neatly in place. Others concentrated only on the top row, the more prestigious, of his ribbons. Although unaware of the deeds he had performed, they knew these awards were not easily earned and they were presented, usually, for actions in combat.

Though most people ignored the "Expert" in shooting badge, an award as rare as a paper clip, they all admired the other unfamiliar medal, gleaming on his chest. This medal, a silver litter carrying a medical cross and caduceus, surrounded by a wreath, was his proudest achievement. It was the Combat Medic Badge. He

pretended not to notice as others scanned
his uniform and nodded their heads after
"reading" his military history. One person
who studied his uniform could not be
ignored.

Hours ago, as the bus had lumbered
away from one of countless stops, an
elderly man wearing a black "WWII
VETERAN" cap slowly made his way down
the aisle and stopped at the empty seat
beside Eiric. He had passed other empty
seats and there were still more behind this
one, but he apparently liked what he saw.
He smiled at Eiric and yelled, "Combat
Medic!" Eiric smiled back as the man
settled into the chair beside him. Tufts of
tangled gray hair poked out of the opening
of his unbuttoned Hawaiian shirt. Pale legs
were exposed, trapped between the bottom
hem of his khaki shorts and the tops of his
mid-calf dress socks. He was cheerful
despite looking terribly uncomfortable, as
his tall frame was forced to cram into a
space made for someone half his size.

Without introduction, the man started a
one-sided conversation. He told Eiric that

he had served as an infantryman in the war in Germany, but he had seen little combat as he had been deployed shortly before VE day. His son, however, had not been as lucky in Vietnam. He also had been a grunt but was seriously wounded on his second tour of duty.

"A combat medic, colored feller like yerself, saved my boy's life." Eiric's jaw clenched, but quickly relaxed as he realized the man was not trying to be offensive, it was just his way of describing a black man. As he listened, the man had nothing but praise for the colored medic that saved his son.

"Yessir, Johnny, that's my son, was pinned down pretty good. He could see the rounds chewin' away at the brush around him. He said he looked down at the blood shootin' out his leg, so he called for help. He saw a couple of his buddies lookin' up the hill at him, shakin' their heads and wavin' at him.

"At the time, he thought they were sayin' their goodbyes, but he found out a few seconds later they were just tellin' him to be quiet and stay put. He saw some plants movin' but didn't pay it any mind, at first, since they were already bein' moved by the bullets comin' at him. He was reachin' for his leg when he saw two small, white dots and a thin sliver of white beneath them. He realized that he was lookin' at a pair of eyes when the thin line turned into a big ol' smile on the face of this Colored, crawlin' up the hill towards him. You know what that man did when he got to my Johnny?

"He patched up Johnny's leg, started an IV on him, give him something for the pain, morphine, I 'spect. Then, he tied a rope around him and the other end around hisself and pulled my son back down the hill into a clearin' that was sheltered from the enemy fire. They were able to take care of John and get him evac'ed to an aid station.

"Oh, did I tell you? The medic took two rounds, one in the arm and one in the rear while he was crawlin' down that hill, towin' my boy on a stretch of rope. Not one of them white boys tried to go up and save

Johnny. He likes to say they did their best
to return fire, coverin' the medic. You know
what I think? I think the good Lord put that
black feller there and he was the only one
that could have made it up that hill. He was
naturally camouflaged. Hell, Johnny didn't
even see him until he was almost on top of
him and then not even 'til he smiled! I don't
know about you, but that's what I call a
hero! But you already know what I'm
talkin' about, because I see that Combat
Medic Badge you're wearin'. They don't
just hand those out, you saved somebody,
didn't you?"

Eiric nodded in silence. "Desert Storm,
right?" Again, Eiric nodded. The man
extended his right hand and squeezed
firmly as Eiric gave him his hand. "I'm
proud to have met you, Specialist Lesson."
The man continued to talk until he reached
his stop. When the door opened, he
thanked Eiric for his service and as he
stood to exit, he yelled to the rest of the
bus. "Y'all, take a good look at this young
man! He's a real American hero! Every one
of you, Black, White, Mexican, whatever,

should be proud of him and you ought to let him know before either of you get off this damn bus!" He shook Eiric's hand one last time before he departed.

Hours had passed since Johnny's father got off the bus. Eiric couldn't remember his name, but he would never forget him. He was thinking about the old man as the bus came to a stop at the Greensboro station. The sound of the opening door knocked the picture of the older man from Eiric's mind as he hurriedly rose to gather his things. After claiming his bags, Eiric made his way to the ticketing desk to get information on his connection to Murfsburg.

"Three more hours! Please, tell me you're joking? Three more hours until the next bus comes for Murfsburg?"

The man behind the counter stepped back from his desk as the soldier yelled at him. Over the years, he had become accustomed to this kind of outburst but the menacing visage of the enraged soldier before him made him long for the days when he had managed a local bakery. He looked at Eiric's face then at his uniform and wondered how many people he had killed to get so many ribbons. Eiric, taking note of the man's fear, regained his composure and spoke in a quiet tone.

"Don't worry about it, Man. I'll just call my mom and have her pick me up. I can't wait three hours to go another twenty miles. Where are the phones I can use?" The man pointed to a wall behind Eiric across the terminal. Eiric thanked him and headed off for the phones.

About half an hour after his phone call, Eiric's parents arrived, along with his sister and brother. He stood a little taller as they approached him and stuck his chest out a little more. After a warm reception filled with hugs, jokes, and praise over his uniform, they loaded up in their van and left the station behind.

His family talked on the way home, updating him on all the changes and the local gossip. Eiric smiled, nodded, or grunted as needed, but mostly just looked out the windows as they passed familiar landmarks. With very few exceptions, everything was still the same as it was when he left years ago. In his mind, Eiric said things like: *That place is still here? Oh yeah, I remember that. Man, that guy is standing in the same spot he was standing in four years ago! Wearing the same clothes! Nothing's changed, except a few new buildings. It's like time never touched this place.*

Eventually, he saw the sign for the city limit of Murfsburg. His father was driving through town instead of taking the more direct route home. He wanted Eiric to see the new bowling alley. Eiric just wanted to get home and out of his uniform. He shifted a couple of times in his seat. They passed the bowling alley and he flatly said, "Nice." Some friends from church drove by and honked their horn. Eiric ground his teeth. As they drove closer to downtown, he loosened his tie. Beads of barely visible sweat formed on his brow.

The van turned onto Main St. and Eiric's nostrils began to flare. Everyone else continued to talk but all Eiric could hear was his own quickening respirations. The sound of the air passing in and out of his nose drowned out the sound of his pounding heart. He couldn't hear it, but he felt each thump in his chest, jack–hammering its way through his shirt and jacket. He looked at his family to see if they felt the beats or heard his raspy breathing, but they continued to fill him in on all he had missed in their small town.

Eiric wiped his forehead and felt the pulsing lines of the bulging blood vessels. His eyes began to dart from his passenger window to the front windshield. An object ahead, faint at first, gradually became clearer as they passed building after familiar building. Eiric focused on one of these store fronts, a gift card shop, as he felt the car come to a stop. He did not want to look away from this store but something inside him compelled him to look ahead. Eiric held his breath as he jerked his head forward to glare at the object outside the front windshield.

There, on an island of flowers, surrounded by a circular roadway, was a granite pedestal. Atop the rectangular base, stood a stallion, his deadly charge frozen in stone, as his rider, a Confederate soldier with a look of longing, pointed the tip of his sword to the south.

Eiric's father engaged the engine, easing past the yield sign and into the circular drive around the monument. As the van rolled smoothly along, Eiric's gaze remained fixed on the statue. As they exited the circle, and the statue faded away, Eiric began to breathe again.

Murfsburg

Days had passed since Eiric's return home. Settling into civilian life was becoming an unexpected chore. Although he had turned his alarm clock off, he still found himself waking up before five every morning. This morning upon rising, he sat on the edge of his bed trying to adjust to the details of his surroundings. Sitting there, blind in the dark, strange noises, made by things unseen, crept into his ears. He clamped his eyelids shut and began to put names to the sounds. Over his bed, he heard a quiet hum. A faint, cool breeze on his face assured him that the sound above his head came from the slowly spinning ceiling fan.

Beyond the walls and closed door of his room, a short-lived rustling let him know that someone else turned over in bed. Next, he heard a tapping, and then a metallic clank. There was a momentary pause followed by a hissing noise. Eiric angled his head and held his breath to better focus on these sounds. Again, the tapping came to him, along with more hissing. He looked around the room and spotted two dark shapes on the floor. He reached out and snatched them up. The unidentified shapes turned immediately into a T-shirt and shorts. He eased them on and slipped silently out of bed towards the hissing sound.

The whole house was dark, except for the light in the kitchen, which always remained on. As he inched his way towards the kitchen, other sounds, easily recognized, came to him. A ticking clock. A faucet dripping. The buzz of the refrigerator, and the scuffle of...slippers? He froze in his tracks as the tapping, louder now, suddenly started and stopped.

A long, distorted, gray ghost glided across the wall in front of him. It floated quickly across the wall before melting into the shadows. He could feel the lids of his eyes stretching to their max. There was the hissing sound again! Eiric forced his eyes closed and concentrated on the sound. It wasn't a hiss, it was a... sizzle. Something was sizzling! Immediately, a strong aroma of hickory and heated swine wafted to his flexing nostrils. The next sound to hit his eardrums was his own voice. "Hmmm! Bacon!" Eiric completed the short walk to the kitchen where his mother was busy preparing breakfast.

"Morning, Lil Boy! I didn't wake you up, did I?"

"Morning Mama. Naw, I was already up. Habit, I guess. Why are you up so early?" He squinted at the time display on the microwave. "It's just after four thirty."

Eiric's mother shrugged her shoulders and an uneasy smile appeared on her face as she replied, "Trouble sleeping." Eiric wasn't sure if she was asking or telling him, so he shoved a strip of bacon in his mouth and grunted. "What's wrong, Eiric?" Having no clue what his mother meant, he jerked his head back and stared blankly. Again, he grunted. Eiric's mother took a seat across from him and continued to talk. "Listen, we're all very happy you're home, but I've got to ask you something. I'm worried about you. Every night since you came home, your father and I wake up because we hear you screaming and crying, fighting, like something is after you. I can't imagine the stuff you've been through." She paused before finally asking, "Do you need some kind of help, like a counselor, or maybe some medication?"

Eiric shook his head, avoiding her gaze. "No, Mama, I don't need any help. I don't know what you're talking about. I don't remember any dreams, and I think I would know if I was screaming, or anything, at night. I feel fine. Besides, I already talked to a counselor on post, and she said bad dreams are normal after being in stressful situations like combat."

"So, you were having nightmares?"

Eiric blinked hard. "None I can recall. A lot of people had to go see a therapist when we got back. They even came to our units with the chaplains to make sure everybody knew they had someone to talk to, that they were not alone. Everybody went through the same," *shit*, he thought, "stuff," he said.

"Well, I'm glad you talked to somebody. I just wanted you to know that we love you and we're here if you need anything." She returned to her cooking, leaving Eiric seated with a head full of thoughts. He felt bad lying to her. Well, maybe he hadn't lied as much as he had left out some of the truth.

Therapists had gone out to the different combat units to talk with groups of soldiers, explaining that there was no shame in seeking help, and outlining their programs. Surveys were filled out, compiled and analyzed. Some soldiers who had participated were invited to join groups to discuss their feelings. An even smaller few were 'stongly encouraged,' a nice way of being **ordered**, to go in for one-on-one sessions with a therapist. Eiric was one of the few.

Eiric's mind drifted back several weeks as he recalled the last time he had been asked about his dreams. Reluctantly, and full of apprehension, he had gone to the office of Mental Hygiene. His presence was requested after several of his fellow soldiers had expressed their fears that he was going crazy.

Wutdafuck? Some mothafuckahs with **real** *mothafuckin' problems gave these Soft-talking motherfuckers my name so they would leave them the fuck alone! So, what, I'm supposed to come in and cry, and then these buttfucks can call me a crazy fuck and kick me out of the fuckin' Army! Then, that sort of fucks me out of school and stuck in some motherfuckin' dead-end job, if I'm lucky enough to get that motherfuckah! Man, fuck that!*

The Soft-talkers were good. They sent in a young, pretty, female sergeant, with a soothing voice to interview him. Eiric responded to the line of questions about his reported outbreaks during the night as best as he could. He admitted knowledge of the dreams, but only because others had told him about his crying in the night.

If what they said was true, shouldn't I remember it? Shouldn't I at least be tired, or bothered? Instead, he felt great, refreshed, and looked forward to doing his job and having fun with his friends. He had ended the session by telling the young lady that he couldn't control his dreams, but, more importantly, his dreams couldn't control him. He was sent back to his unit with the assurance that everything was normal, which was exactly what he thought...until he arrived back at his unit.

From that point on, Eiric's Platoon Sergeant, a woefully inept NCO, whose incompetence was highlighted repeatedly during the war, attempted to become his best friend. Sergeant First Class, *asshole*, Matthew was the first person to welcome Lesson back from his appointment, literally, with open arms. He had even adopted the same sing-song lilt in his voice as the Soft-talkers.

Suspicion forced Eiric's eyebrows to arch almost up to his hairline at SFC Matthew's first word.

"Eiric!"

What? this muthafuckah never uses anybody's first name!

"How you doin', Son?"

Hold up, hold up! I have a father! I don't want anybody mistaking me for your son, with your sorry ass!

"Tell you what," Matthew continued, "why don't you just take the rest of the day off. That work detail I had you on can wait. I can just get somebody else to do it. You go rest, Son." SFC Matthew was doing his best to mimic the Soft-talkers but the effect was odd. He seemed pained, like he was battling constipation, as he spoke these words. He even managed a smile, but to Eiric he looked like a cornered opossum.

Yeah, something is definitely wrong. SFC Matthew was not a man known for his compassion. He never missed an opportunity to give his people demeaning tasks. He was better known for his unique ability to kiss his superiors' butts while breaking the backs of his subordinates. All ranks were aware that he thoroughly enjoyed both talents.

Later that day, Skippy informed Eiric that SFC Matthew had received a phone call from Eiric's counselor. She had called while he was returning to his unit following their talk. She had advised SFC Matthew to take it easy on Lesson. This request was not received well by Matthew, who began to curse at the therapist on the phone. The profanity attracted the attention of Skippy, who was just passing Matthew's office. It also caught the ear of Captain Crest, the Medical Officer at the Mental Hygiene clinic. Skippy continued to eavesdrop, enjoying the transformation from arrogant, profane bully to subdued, compliant, brown-noser, as CPT Crest ripped SFC Matthew a, much needed, new one.

After these encounters, Eiric refused to discuss anything about dreams, or the war, with anyone. Eiric reflexively grunted as he became aware that his mother was asking him about his plans for the day. Between grunts, he answered her with a vague, "I'm gonna get a job."

His mother talked excitedly about possible places for him to apply as she continued to cook. He watched his mom and wondered how many times she had prepared meals for her family. She seemed to derive pleasure from preparing meals for others. He dismissed the thought that she would ever consider this to be work, or that she was doing the chores of a servant or a... slave.

He paused as that word stuck in his head. He saw the image of a weary woman, stooped over with age and hard labor. Her forehead was wrinkled from her toil on earth as her eyes sought Heaven. Her knuckles were swollen by "Arthur" and chalked from constantly cleaning behind other people. He felt guilty for thinking of his mother as a slave, so he went over to the sink and started washing dishes.

He told her it was okay, that he wanted to help, as she tried to stop him, reminding him that, "A good cook always cleans up their mess." He finished the dishes and turned around as she was preparing plates. Nobody else was awake, but their plates would be ready to heat in the microwave later. The others would have no problem nuking their food, but not his father. He would come in, insist on his hot coffee but stuff his face with cold food, despite his wife's protests. He always claimed food tasted better cold, after the flavors settled in.

Eiric watched his mother work and he heard the words coming from his mouth before he could stop them. "Mama, how do you feel about the monument downtown? I mean, has it ever bothered you?" He couldn't believe he had asked her this. It was a subject nobody ever really talked about. He saw that she tensed momentarily before she forced a smile and controlled her answer.

"How do I feel about the monument?" she echoed. "Well, before I die I'd like to blow it to pieces!" This statement, coming from his gentle, church-going mother, caught him off guard. "All my life, I wished somebody would use some dynamite or crash a big truck into Ol' Reb and knock him off into a million pieces! Of course, I don't want anybody to get hurt in the process. It would be nice to see him and his horse in a pile of rubble nobody could put back together. Why did you ask me about Ol' Reb? You're not planning on blowing him up, are you?"

This she asked with a sly smile betraying a glimmer of hope. Eiric laughed,

"Naw, I'm not gonna blow him up! I really don't care about 'Ol' Reb.' Matter of fact, until you just said it, I never knew he had a name."

"Oh, yeah, Chile! That's what my grandma called him, so, that's what I've called him all my life! I'm surprised you never heard me."

He shook his head. "Never heard you call him by name." *I did see you roll your eyes at him.* "So, what's the horse's name?"

She blinked hard for a few seconds before responding, "'Ol' Reb's Horse', I guess!" They both laughed as they picked up their plates. The conversation changed to other topics, like the weather, their dogs, and other folks' business.

After breakfast, Eiric cleaned up their dishes, then went to his room and prepared to go out on his quest for a job. A civilian job. The Army had been his first real job. Before that, he mowed lawns, cleaned barns, and helped an older, family friend detail cars on the weekends. He wanted to get started right away. It was still early but he had a lot of stops to make. In addition to applying for jobs, he also needed to register for nursing school. With his background in the Army, along with an outstanding high school transcript, Eiric knew he would have no problem being accepted into the program at the local community college. After all, he had been in the top of his class, and excelled in advanced courses, earning him a spot in the *Who's Who of American Students,* as well as the honor of being named a NC Scholar, which was awarded to students who maintained high GPA's.

I remember pissing everybody off, my folks, my teachers, my friends when I told them I was going in the Army instead of accepting those scholarships. Maybe they were right, maybe I should have gone on to college, first. Who knows where I might be right now if I had listened to them instead of going in the service. I could be well on my way to becoming a surgeon by now. Or, maybe doing something in research, who knows? Anyway, that's hypothetical. I'm happy with my choice because I got to see the world and made some great friends. I haven't even seen any of my old high school friends since graduation. Plus, I have lots of adventures to tell everybody about.

Eiric's breathing faltered with that thought. He was wide awake but he suddenly found himself trapped in a dream that seemed all too real.

He was looking down at the sand outside his humvee window as the earth rolled slowly by. He could hear the leader of the Scouts on the radio urging his troops to move ahead faster. He also heard the response of the Platoon Sergeant, pleading with his boss to allow the platoon to continue at their sluggish pace so they could get their bearings.

A massive sandstorm, which had obscured their vision all morning, had just died down, allowing the Scouts to use their best tools; their eyes. As good as the high-tech gadgets were at helping them maneuver towards their objective, nothing beat having eyes on whatever lie in front of you.

Eiric placed a lifesaver candy in his mouth and peered out his window. The Scout vehicles formed a skirmish line, each vehicle about 75 meters apart from the next, travelling ahead of the main body of combat vehicles, Abrams tanks and Bradley fighting vehicles. Their mission was to blaze the best route of passage for the battalion and to report any hostile encounters along the way. Ordinarily, the Scouts would have been 1 to 2 kilometers in front of the tanks however, the sandstorm had caused a major slow down. Also, the Scouts had slowed even more to allow the Platoon Sergeant's vehicle to rejoin them after an unplanned trip to the Aid Station that morning.

Earlier that morning, while the Scouts were checking out the tents of some nomadic goat herders, one of the Scouts had developed crushing chest pain accompanied by shortness of breath. Fearing an impending cardiac event, Eiric, also known as Doc, had made the call to transport the Scout back to the Aid Station to be checked out by the doctor. The Platoon Leader had put up a weak protest but was shut down by the Platoon Sergeant who trusted Doc's judgment.

They loaded Willis into the humvee, giving the others the okay to continue forward after clearing the village. After radioing back to HQ, *Samurai 2,* the Platoon Sergeant's vehicle, headed back to the Aid Station. It had been relatively easy, going in the same direction as the blowing sand, traveling back towards the supply trains. They first drove through the columns of tanks. Next, they passed the Bradley fighting vehicles. Soon, the heavy equipment of the Engineers came into view. Finally, they made their way into the ranks of the HQ vehicles, and guided by their GPS, made a beeline for the rolling Aid Station.

The back door of the APC lowered, forming a ramp. The Physician's Assistant, Chief Jinks, met them at the foot of the ramp, receiving a quick report from Eiric as Willis was taken inside the APC and connected to a heart monitor and oxygen. The other medics resupplied Eiric and patted him on the back before he jumped back into *Samurai 2.* The engine roared as they headed back into the rushing maelstrom.

Once again, the stinging sand affected their vision but this time they had an advantage. They had already traversed this pathway twice this morning and they knew this part of Iraq was safe, having been cleared earlier. Aided by the GPS, they sped past the slower moving trucks and armored vehicles whose occupants were seeing, through blinding sand, this area for the first time.

Samurai 2 moved with reckless confidence, their only fear being ramming into the back of a larger vehicle as it materialized from the curtain of sand. After passing the last of the Engineers' oversized vehicles, they drove through a deserted area for a while before coming up to the Bradley APC's. They waved as they cut through their lines and the Bradley drivers gave them the thumbs-up. Soon, they were leaving the Brads behind and entering another dead area free of traffic.

They moved swiftly over the dunes, cresting the peaks and roller-coasting down the opposite sides. Tension mounted as they made out the backs of the tanks.

Somehow, they had made it to the tanks too soon after leaving the Bradleys. Their formations were too close. This could be deadly if the enemy engaged, for they would be too bunched up, easier targets. Fortunately, if there were enemy troops nearby, they also would be affected by the sandstorm.

The humvee, looking like a toy next to the tanks, finally broke through their line and headed out into new territory, all alone. Eiric was doing his best to scan outside his window. He sat behind the driver, so he watched the left flank as the driver looked ahead. SGT Hach was in the gunner's ring up top and scanned right and forward and back. The Platoon Sergeant looked right and forward and kept them on track with the GPS. He also monitored the radio. Each man did his best to focus, ignoring the pain as they kept vigil for the enemy.

Suddenly, they were back in line with the Scouts. The column halted as the leaders spoke over the radio. They all agreed that the lines were too close together. The fighting vehicles were ordered to slow down and the Scouts were ordered to speed up. As the command was given, and the Scouts began to move forward, the sandstorm fizzled revealing a clear landscape in all directions.

He was looking down at the sand outside his humvee window as they crept forward. He shouted out a report to the Platoon Sergeant after placing his last lifesaver in his mouth. "Sergeant Hughes, I've got tubes sticking out of the ground! Looks like air tubes coming up out of the ground!"

The Scouts stopped as SFC Hughes passed the report over the radio. The driver, Gennard, turned to Eiric after he too saw the pieces of cut off PVC protruding from the sand. He shook his head and turned his gaze back to the front windshield. To their far left, rose a railroad embankment. In front, to their right, were several conical dunes in orderly rows, approximately 10 feet high, each. These were not natural, and SFC Hughes reported them to the lieutenant, requesting more time for further investigation. The request was promptly denied and they were once again ordered to move forward at combat speed.

SFC Hughes slammed down the receiver and cursed. He yelled to his crew, "They're trying to kill us! They want us to drive into an ambush! Stay sharp!"

Lesson looked away from the Platoon Sergeant who had, until this moment, been a source of strength, their very own John Wayne. Now, he was just like the rest of them...afraid.

Eiric looked out his window and scanned beyond the hood of *Samurai 3*, the next vehicle on their left flank. Bordering them, just past the last vehicle in their line-up, rose the low railroad berm. He could hear the rattles and clanks of the armored vehicles to their rear. They were still too close!

Great! Either we rush into an ambush or we get blasted by our own tanks. Either way, the Scouts lose! ***We*** *lose.* Eiric's moment of reflection was interrupted by Gennard's frantic voice.

"What the fu... Contact! I've got contact at 12 o'clock! Dismount at 12 o'clock!" Eiric's head snapped forward and he saw what Gennard pointed out. In the distance, a lone figure stood facing them.

The body, too far away to distinguish facial features, leaned over at the waist raising his hands to his mouth. The figure straightened with one hand raised to shield his eyes. Then he quickly bent over again with both hands at his mouth. He had spotted the Scouts and was informing his buddies who were still below ground. Those were the man's last words. SFC Hughes had called in the enemy contact as the man was bending over the first time. Now, the tanks behind the Scouts made a new sound, like stripping gears in a car with manual transmission.

Eiric thrust his arm out his window and pointed to the soldier in front of them. As they passed the parked Scout vehicles, the turbo engines of the tanks screamed mechanical war cries. At last, they were able to perform the task they were designed for. The sounds of war,

explosions, gunfire, and juggernaut engines
all flooded Eiric's ears. There was room,
though, for one more unwanted sound.

"**Medic!** We need Doc, *Samurai 3's* been
hit!" Eiric looked left and saw plumes of
smoke rising from the hood of the humvee.
Gennard looked back to make sure no more
tanks were driving past before turning the
vehicle to their left flank. As they
approached the crippled *Samurai 3*,
something on the ground on the far side of
the vehicle came into view. Three Scouts
were surrounding the fallen body of their
driver. He lay in the sand and could have
been mistaken for a sunbather on a beach.
It could have been a day at the beach except
for the exploding shells, the screaming, and
all the blood covering his body. Eiric's eyes
widened as he looked down at his friend,
dying in the sand.

In his bedroom, Eiric shouted, "No!'"
and the dream was over. He was shaking
and covered in sweat. The dream, or vision,
or memory only lasted a few seconds but it
took him awhile to get over it.

A knock on the door, accompanied by his mother's voice, let him know he was safe at home, but her concerned tone reminded him of scared soldiers outside his room in the barracks. He couldn't bear the thought of her being afraid of him, so he had to lie to her. "Did you want something?" she asked.

"Uh, I thought I heard you ask me if I wanted something else to eat! I'm alright!" He wiped away at the sweat as he listened to her walk away. He looked at his hands clutching the towel and noticed that they were trembling. Before he could stop himself, he was crying. He bit into a corner of the towel and dove into his closet to mask the sound.

In his head, he could hear himself scream. He shoved more of the towel, as much as he could, into his mouth and covered his ears, rocking himself until the screaming stopped. When he had calmed down, he lay down on his side, halfway inside his closet, with a pair of running shoes for a pillow. He was exhausted and the pain at his temples was nauseating. He pulled the towel from his mouth and slept soundly for two hours.

His mother's knock at the door, reminding him of his plans for the day, forced him to his feet. He thanked her, stating, "I must have dozed off," before hitting the shower again. Outside the bathroom door, Eiric's mother let a tear roll down her cheek before she returned to her own bedroom.

Eiric finished getting dressed and, armed with several copies of his resume, headed out into the world of job hunting. He removed the cover from his red mustang and looked at it a long time. It was a gift he had bought for himself when he first joined the Army. His father had taken care of it for him while he was away, only driving it on the weekends. The car was almost paid off and in new condition. He had managed to save some money and he had a car that he loved thanks to careful spending while in the military. He folded the cover and placed it in the trunk. He then got inside and started the engine, enjoying the sound before easing it out of the driveway. He merged into traffic and headed to Greensboro, first.

He applied at several hospitals, clinics, and doctor's offices. He even applied at nursing homes, which he really didn't want to work in. He drove all around Greensboro before returning to Murfsburg to do the same.

In Murfsburg, Eiric also applied for the county's EMS. At each place he applied, he was greeted by friendly faces that thanked him for his service and assured him he would be considered for an interview. He felt optimistic as he drove to the community college. It was at this place he received the first blow to his ego.

After filling out his application and providing his transcript, he was ushered to the office of the Dean of Nursing. She was an attractive older woman in her forties, who became less attractive as she told him it would be two years before he could start, due to an existing waiting list. He was crushed. He tried to argue that he was a better candidate due to his years of practical experience. The Dean was not moved. He thanked her for her time and walked back to his car.

Two years before I can go to school. Well, at least I won't have to worry about money. The GI Bill will go a long way here. I'll just take her advice and knock out my prerequisite courses in the meantime. Hopefully, I won't get sidetracked before the two years are up.

He drove off with nagging thoughts in his head of unemployment, unwanted pregnancies, accidents, jail...anything that would keep him from going to school. He eased off the gas and placed both hands on the wheel as he attempted to ward off the imagined stumbling blocks.

Eiric drove aimlessly for a long while until he noticed a dull ache creeping into his shoulders. He pulled into an open bay at a car wash and left the engine running. Focusing on all he had accomplished this day, he tried to ignore the pain. He knew this mind trick would not work because he had felt this pain before and it was only a preface to real agony about to begin. He reclined his seat and prepared for the worst.

In minutes, his prediction was proven accurate. A sharp sensation, like a burning sword cutting slowly into his flesh, drove deep into the sockets connecting his arms to his torso. Next, two distinct feelings alternated, in no uniform pattern, from one shoulder to the next. While one shoulder felt like an impacted wisdom tooth surrounded by ice chips, the other was tortured by an invisible rusty saw, cutting back and forth, each tooth of the blade catching on a new nerve resulting in a unique blend of pain and nausea. Eiric shrugged his shoulders and held his arms close to his chest, whimpering and praying for an end to the pain. Included in his prayer, was a request that nobody would see him like this. The pain continued, intensified, and he screamed without restraint.

Minutes later, his prayers were answered. The pain in his shoulders released him but he knew it would someday return. He raised the back of his seat and got out of his car. As he walked to the change machine, he was relieved to find empty bays all along the length of the car wash.

Eiric returned home well after dark, intentionally missing dinner with his family. For some reason, he felt uncomfortable if they looked at him for any length of time. Maybe they could tell that he couldn't take his pains like a man. Perhaps they could see the horrors he had witnessed and placed the blame for all the carnage on him. Probably, they had heard his screams in the night, and like the blunt, uncaring soldiers he had lived with, decided that something was off, that he, "Wasn't right."

Whatever the reason, he found it increasingly difficult to look his family in the eye. *They know the truth. I'm a coward that went to war.* He took his time covering his car, allowing even more time for his family to clear the front rooms, before he finally went inside. When he entered the house, all heads turned towards him from the dinner table. They had waited for him to start dinner.

He tried to gauge their thoughts by their expressions, thinly veiled behind wisps of steam rising from their plates. His sister showed all her teeth as she grinned at him. He thought, *oh, you think it's funny? I hurt now, for no reason, and it's a joke?*

His brother shook his head, looked at his watch, and shoved a piece of bread into his mouth. *I'm sorry, are you hungry? Am I keeping you from filling your face? At least you know you're gonna get a hot meal! Why don't you try eating MRE's day in and day out while on patrol! Besides, I didn't ask you to wait for me!*

He looked at his father, who immediately turned to his wife and asked if they could start now. *So, you're embarrassed to even look at me? I'm sorry I'm not in my uniform! Sorry I didn't get more medals or kill anybody!*

His mother urged Eiric to come have a seat. *Thanks for showing your poor baby some pity. That's all I need, another Soft-talker! Or another SFC Matthew!* He sat down with his family and stared at his plate.

He began to feel guilty for the angry thoughts that seemed to spring from nowhere. *I'm a jerk! There's no way they know what kind of day I've had. Where do these thoughts come from? I never thought stuff like this before, I always made a joke out of everything. Why do I get so angry, now?*

He apologized for being late and for not being able to start in the nursing program at the next semester. His brother laughed and Eiric shot him a deadly glance. He saw his hands wrapped around his brother's throat, squeezing tight. *There I go again! Lord, help me! Please!*

His brother smiled uneasily and said, "Man, you don't have to apologize to us about anything. You're a hero! If the school is making you wait, that's their loss. Hey, I saw your boy, Jerry, and I told him you were home. He wants you to hang out with him, Friday. Hey, since you're his friend, maybe you can tell him to cut that mullet! I thought white dudes stopped wearing those in the 80's? Anyway, I told him to call you later." Eiric nodded quietly. In his head, he apologized for the look he had given his brother and the feeling that went along with it.

Eiric's mother spoke next. "Well, I know you're disappointed about college, but I have some good news for you. While you were out, you got a call. They want you to come in for an interview! I told them you were out taking care of business, and they said they understood, but they really want to talk to you. I thought you would be home before their office closed, but..."

"Who called, who's the interview with?" Eiric interrupted.

"The county called. The director of the county EMS called. They want to see you tomorrow if you can go."

"That is good news. It's great news!" he said. "Of course, I can go talk to them! I can't believe I got a call from the job I really wanted the most on the first day!"

Eiric's father said, in a solemn tone, "Be careful with those people, Eiric. I don't know if I completely trust them."

"What do you mean? They're paramedics. I'll be working for 911!"

"Yeah, well, you just watch yourself. I'm sure in this whole county, there had to be at least one person who wasn't white that was qualified to do what they do.

"I mean, before you came home. Maybe I'm wrong. Maybe nobody black has applied before. Maybe they were just waiting for you to come back and apply. Who knows? It would be nice to see a Black face step off one of those ambulances to help people. I just hope they want you for the right reason."

*Wow, this is just like talking to Gandhi. Is everybody stuck in the 60's? This is **1991**! All that civil rights marching and BS is over, we won!*

"Dad, I think they want me because they looked at my resume and liked what they saw. Believe it or not, I am a good medic. All I want to do is help people. This is what I was made for."

"Oh, I know that," his father answered. "I know that's what God put you on this planet to do. You're a better man than me."

Eiric swallowed hard. "There's no way I could deal with people being that hurt or dying and keep my head together. I just hope these paramedics see the same thing in you that we see and they're not just using you."

"Well, even if their intention is to use me, I'll do my job and show them I know my stuff. So, they'll 'use' me and I get to take care of people in my community. It's a win-win situation."

The rest of the meal strayed away from this topic as the others talked about events in their day. Eiric was relieved to no longer be the center of attention. After dinner, he excused himself to prepare for his interview. He went to the bathroom and looked closely in the mirror.

Since coming home, he had given up on shaving daily, enjoying the look of the neatly trimmed, previously unauthorized beard. Tonight, he noticed something he hadn't before. A bald place, completely devoid of hair, showed on his chin like a small island in a sea of black stubble. He knew he had not cut this design on his face.

It looked out of place and he wondered how he had missed seeing it before. Fascinated, he placed a finger on the area and was amazed at how smooth it was. *That's strange,* he thought. After rubbing it a little longer, he grabbed his razor and shaved his face, ridding himself of his fledgling beard, and solving the problem of the missing hair.

After choosing an outfit to wear the next day, he went to bed. As he made himself comfortable, he reflected on the day's activities. His head was full and he hoped the bad thoughts wouldn't spill over to his dreams. On this night, Eiric did not dream. He slept peacefully, unaware that his mother stood outside his door, relieved to hear only snoring from inside the room.

The morning of the interview, Eiric woke up early, as usual. He got dressed and sat in front of a mirror practicing for his interview. He thought of all the possible questions that might be thrown at him. He stared himself in the eye as he delivered his responses. After hours of rehearsing, he set off for the office where he was directed to go. He arrived early, of course, and after

meeting one of the directors, was taken to a
conference room to wait for the rest of the
staff. He didn't have to wait long.

The door opened to reveal five
uniformed men, the Director of EMS, the
Training Officer, and three shift
supervisors, who quickly took turns
shaking his hand before taking their seats
in front of him. After introducing
themselves, they began to ask their
questions. He was totally unprepared for
what they asked.

They did not ask him why he wanted the
job or why he thought he should be hired.
They didn't ask him about his qualifications
or how he would handle a stressful
situation. They only wanted to know about
the war. Did he see any action, was he
scared, did he shoot anybody?

*Did I shoot anybody? Why does
everybody ask that?* They listened to his
account of the war, at least the parts he felt
comfortable describing, with intense
curiosity. They all seemed pleased with his
answers until he said that he did not injure
or kill anyone. They smiled politely and

told him he probably did the right thing, but he could tell that they wanted to hear him say he ripped off someone's head.

Eventually, everyone got around to asking that one question, and everyone displayed the same let-down expression and provided the same clichéd responses to show their 'understanding.'

The rest of the "interview" consisted of the supervisors telling Eiric about their own reasons for not being able to join the military, or about their fathers who had served, and about dangerous situations they each had encountered on the "mean streets" of Murfsburg and the surrounding county. Eiric could only smile and nod at each member as they took turns speaking to him.

Though he looked focused on their every word, his mind began to travel. *What am I doing here? I'm trying to get a job and all you want to do is shoot the shit and tell war stories. I need a job and they want to gossip! Great! I guess I'll still have time to go by the hospital and that warehouse to put in apps after I leave here. What a waste of time!* Eiric shook his head and said, "Excuse me?" when he realized one of the supervisors had finally asked him a question.

The large, balding man smiled and repeated his question. "I said, do you know where the *Deluxe Tailor and Uniform* shop is? That's where you'll need to go to get sized for your uniform. You can stop by there when you leave here and Ol' Earl will get you hooked right up! If it's okay with you, we want you to come on in Monday at about 7 am, and get you started on your orientation."

Eiric could not help laughing as he stammered his answer, "Yeah, I mean, yes Sir! I know where the store is and I can definitely be here at zero seven zero zero."

They all laughed and the big man responded, "That's what I'm talking about! I love the way you guys talk! I wish all our staff came from the military!"

Eiric thanked each member for the interview as he shook their hands before leaving the room. He marched out of the building and maintained his military bearing until he drove away. About a block away, he loosened his tie, blasted the music in his car, and let out a long, loud, triumphant yell. Pedestrians shook their heads as he disturbed their peace. He lowered the volume on the stereo as he drove to Earl's store.

The uniform store sold everything from Boy Scout apparel to police gear, like gun holsters and pepper spray. You could also get clothing there for fishing and hunting. The owner, Earl, was a pretty good tailor, offering an alternative to the poorer quality, lower priced but faster service, dry cleaner down the street.

Moments later, he parked his car and headed into the uniform shop. A loud bell jingled as he entered the building. Almost instantly, a tall, slender man with reading glasses resting on the tip of his nose, appeared from a curtained-off room behind the cash register. The man, Earl, looked at Eiric over the top of his glasses. He looked Eiric in the eyes then glanced down to his feet and back up to his eyes with only a slight movement of his neck.

Earl cleared his throat before speaking. "So, you're the one. Okay, I think I have something that'll fit you."

"Excuse me, but I haven't even told you what I need," Eiric said in an irritated tone.

"You're here for your EMS gear, rat?" Eiric nodded.

"All ratty then! Jimmy, the fat man," Earl said, spreading his hands far apart, "called to let me know you were on your way over. You're what, five-foot eight, about a-hunnert-sixty pounds, ten-a-have shoe, rat? Again, Eiric nodded. "Then I think I got wutchu need."

Eiric followed Earl to a rack near the center of the room. He watched quietly as the old man moved nimbly through the clothes hanging before him. Earl quickly handed him three sky-blue, buttoned down shirts, two, short-sleeved, the other, long-sleeved. He then produced two pairs of navy slacks followed by a pair of black, steel-toed work shoes. "You can go try these on in there," he directed, pointing to a dressing room in the back.

Eiric took the items and went to the nearest stall. He closed the door behind him and changed into the uniform, starting with the short-sleeved shirt. When he had the entire uniform on, he smiled at his appearance in the mirror.

I almost look like a cop! That old dude knows his stuff, this is a perfect fit. He stopped admiring his reflection when he heard a voice calling to him.

"Hey, come on outta there, lemme see you!" He opened the door and stepped out and found Earl looking at him with an approving eye. The old man held out a black utility belt. "You're gonna need this. It's got a holster for your radio, you know, your walkie-talkie. This little doohickey here," he said, pointing at an attached pouch, "is for your gloves, so you'll always have 'em handy." Eiric accepted the belt and strapped it on his waist. Earl continued to speak. "If you want, you can wear your combat boots with your uniform. They tell me you're a soldier."

"Yes Sir. I have my boots, but these shoes feel okay."

"Good. The only other thing you need is a turnout coat, oh, and a windbreaker." Earl produced a heavy coat adorned with the county EMS logo and lots of reflective tape, similar to the coats worn by the fire department. He also handed Eiric a lightweight, navy blue jacket, with "EMS" written in white letters. "Well, that'll do fur now. You can buy more, later on if something tears or you just want extra." The older man placed his fists on his hips and asked, "Oh, if you don't mind, can I ask you a question?"

"Yes Sir."

"Why are you doing this? I mean, why EMS, in this county?"

"What's that supposed to mean? I'm not supposed to help people in my own community? Look, I was good enough for Uncle Sam, so I think I can handle this."

"I'm sure you can. I was just thinkin', a person such as yourself, could make a lot more money in a larger city. Plus, you wouldn't stand out as much. I've been supplyin' the county forever, and you're the first of your kind I've outfitted."

"You mean soldier?" Eiric asked hopefully.

"Person of color," Earl replied bluntly. "A lot of people around here ain't gone like it. You watch yourself, especially the way you talk to some people when you get on scene. The older people, like my age, might not be as, hmm, progressive as you might like 'em to be. They're not gonna take too kindly to you tellin' 'em what to do or worse, puttin' your hands on a white woman, even if she's not nekitt. Be polite, but keep your eyes open, just like in combat."

Is that a threat? What do you know about combat? "Are you threatening me?"

"Naw, I'm just jawin' atcha, tryin' to give you some advice. You come from a good family, and y'all aint never caused too many problems for anybody. Except when your parents bought that property out at the Crossings. A lot of people, one of 'em bein' one of your new bosses, had their eyes on it. It aint no secret, people were pretty pissed when your folks beat 'em out. Now, those same people are gonna see you climbin' in and out of ambulances, somethin' that's never been done around here. Watch yourself is all I'm saying."

"How do you know my parents? You don't even know me."

"This is a small town. Talk gets around faster than corn through a duck! Hell, people have been talkin' about you since you were in grade school. It shouldn't be a surprise that you're doin' what you're doin', but some people are a little slower in the thinkin' department."

"Okay, whatever, so you think you know me. I think you're wrong about the way people are going to react to me. You know, this is 1991. We do have black doctors and nurses that actually take care of and touch white people! I'm not Martin Luther King, I'm just me, but the good ole boys you're so worried about just hired me to work on their ambulances. If they trust me, and the government trusted me, maybe you should too."

"Son, bein' a doctor or a nurse ain't the same as bein' on the trucks! If I'm in the hospital, and have a mind to, I can call the head nurse and tell her not to give me a minority nurse and they have to honor that. And I get to choose my own doctor, if I don't like who I'm stuck with. But out on the streets, paramedics are like rock stars, no, they're gods! You don't get to choose who comes to help you! They show up, take charge, and save lives! They don't write you a worthless prescription and tell you to, 'Take care,' like most docs do. And they don't need to stan' aroun' with their thumbs in their thinkin' holes, waitin' for a **doctor's order**, unlike nurses! They know what to do and they do it!

"People respect that and they look at paramedics with awe. You'll see it when you guys stop for lunch and people let you pass 'em in line. You'll see when they snap their necks at your table every time your walkie-talkie breaks squelch. When you guys come on scene at a car wreck, you'll see the look of relief in people's eyes when they see y'all comin' at 'em. Then, you'll see a look a doubt when they see **you**! I tell you, people 'round here ain't ready for that."

"Well, thanks for the uniforms, but I don't need the advice. I think you might just be stuck in the past. I hope you don't go into shock or have a heart attack when you see you're wrong, but if you do, call 911. I'll come to your rescue!" Eiric took his belongings, still wearing the EMS uniform, and rushed to his car. He wanted to put the old man's words behind him as fast as he could.

On his way home, the engine roared and the music blared, but all he could hear was Earl. Eiric parked his car and went into his parents' home. *So, everybody wanted this house? Too bad! People are gonna look at me with doubt?* Eiric looked at his approaching family and saw the pride in their eyes. *I don't think so, Mr. Earl.*

Later that evening, Eiric's friend, Jerry, called him to let him know he was going to treat him to a night he wouldn't forget. It had been years since they had seen each other so Eiric was eager to catch up with his childhood friend. Jerry picked him up and they cruised by some of their old hangouts before hitting the clubs.

At each familiar stop, the two shook their heads and scoffed at the new crop of teenagers doing the same silly stuff they had done at their age. Young girls grouped together pretending not to notice the guys showing off on skateboards, wrestling, or just trying to look cool.

"Look at these idiots! Did we act like that?" Jerry asked.

"You did! Look, I think that dude with the mullet stole your dance moves! He even looks like you!" Eiric was pointing at a pimply-faced blond guy, playing air guitar as two of his friends played air drums and sang into invisible mics. "Yeah, he could be your twin, or your long-lost son."

"Okay, and that's you over there, getting shot down, as usual, by that cutie you know you never had a chance with," Jerry replied, pointing towards two young ladies who were holding each other as they laughed at some poor nerd turning away from them in shame.

Eiric looked where Jerry directed and said, "Daaang! That reminds me of the time I asked Tracey to go to the prom with me.

She was like, 'Not you!' Then she called Carol Meeks over, told her what I said, and they both laughed their asses off. Man, I was devastated."

"That's what you get for going after the hottest black girl in our class." Eiric looked away from his friend as the words, "Hottest black girl," echoed in his head. "Don't worry, Eiric, where we're going tonight, nobody's gonna turn you down. They have a few black girls for you. Shoot, a couple of them look so good, I don't care if they are black, I would go for them."

Eiric pushed back into his seat, grinding his teeth. *Where did that come from? We've been friends since kindergarten and I never heard you make comments like that. You do realize I'm black?*

They continued to talk as Jerry drove to the mystery destinations. He informed Eiric that he was still working in the local factory, a job he got right out of high school thanks to his father. It wasn't the greatest job in the world but it paid his bills. After talking about the routine problems at his job he asked Eiric about his time in the

Army. Eiric told him he really liked the friends he had made and about all the historic places he had been in Europe, but Jerry was only interested in one thing.

"Did you shoot anybody?"

Wow, always this question. "Naw, Jerry, I didn't shoot anybody." Jerry rolled his eyes as he continued to look over the steering wheel. Eiric considered his friend for a moment. *He's my best friend. If I can't tell him about what happened over there, who can I talk to?* Jerry's look of disappointment changed as Eiric decided to talk.

"I almost shot two people, one was an old man and the other was a kid. They were in the wrong place at the wrong time and I almost killed them. The Army would have said it was okay, that we were at war, but, I know it would have been murder. I think about those faces and I thank God I didn't pull the trigger."

He went into greater detail surrounding the circumstances, deeper than he had intended. Jerry was a good listener and Eiric couldn't stop talking to his oldest and best friend about things he swore he wouldn't tell anyone. When he finished talking, he was shocked to find that they had been parked for a long time. "I'm sorry, Man, I didn't mean to keep running off at the mouth."

"It's cool, I'm glad you got that stuff out. You saw a lot of action! I can't even imagine it all. Whew, you make it seem a lot different, a lot scarier, than what I was watching on TV. I'm proud of you, Boy! Anyway, let's go on in here. You're gonna love this place!" They got out and Eiric followed Jerry to the entrance where Jerry paid his way in. "Don't worry, I got you on this!"

They went inside the darkened building and the smell of stale cigarette smoke and beer engulfed them. Loud music, full of bass, thumped in their ears. They passed several other guys as they made their way to a small table. They sat down and like everyone else in the place, faced in the same direction. On an elevated stage, in the center of the room, was a chrome pillar adorned with a long-legged, G-string clad, platinum blond beauty with unnaturally large breasts. It was a strip club.

Adding to Eiric's surprise were Jerry's next words. "That's my girl!" He whistled and clapped before adding to her growing collection of cash.

"Man, I thought we were going to a club where we could actually talk to some women, not a jiggly-joint!"

"You can talk to them! I come here almost every night! I know all the girls! Watch, they'll be sitting with us most of the night. And you can meet Amber! I'm gonna marry her, one day! Who knows, you might find a lady you can get with! I told you, there's a few black girls that work here and some of the regular girls are into dating Brothers, so don't worry." The smile on Eiric's face twitched slightly. "And if you can't find something you like here...yeah right...maybe you will at the next place!"

It wasn't long before a group of beautiful women, including the blond, Amber, joined the men at their table. Eiric stared at his friend, amazed that these beautiful women were talking with them, not soliciting money, just talking and enjoying themselves.

My Man, Jerry! How much money do you drop in here? These ladies are sitting here, half-naked, just chillin'! I can't believe this, I'm in heaven!

Eiric smiled as each woman was introduced by his friend. There was Candy, a red-head with large, emerald eyes. A brunette with a blond streak of hair, Tempting, and Delicious, another, short-haired brunette with freckles sat with them. Then there was Erotica, a raven-haired Latina dressed in a black leather bustier.

The last girl to be introduced was a caramel-skinned woman with smoky, dark brown eyes, and long, jet black hair, named Jamaica. She sat closest to Eiric and spoke close to his ear when she talked to him. The combination of her accent and the warmth of her breath on his neck made him blush. She liked that and told him so.

Jerry entertained himself with the others as Eiric talked with Jamaica. He always felt nervous, like his mother would appear to fuss at him at any moment, whenever he went to strip clubs. That's why he only went to them if he was in a group of his friends and it was their idea. He did his best to act confident.

"What's your name? Your real name, if you don't mind?"

"It's Renee, but since I can fake a Jamaican accent..." she smiled as she waved her hand in front of her face. "So, Jerry tells us you're a big hero. I'm impressed." She spoke softly in her normal dialect.

"I'm not a hero, I just did my job. I'm the one that's impressed. You guys are beautiful, I mean, even with your clothes on!" His cheeks warmed as he blushed again. "Sorry, I didn't mean it like that." Renee shrugged her shoulders and waved away his words with her hand. She had heard much worse. "And you're hanging out with us!"

"Look, your friend comes in here every night 'cause he's in love with Amber. She thinks it's cute in a way but kind of pathetic. If her boyfriend was the jealous type, your friend would be dead, but he doesn't care as long as she brings the

money home. And her ass! We always sit
with him because he's harmless and it
keeps us from some of the hardcore
assholes that don't know what 'No' means.
We hang out with him between sets so it
looks like we're busy and the manager
leaves us alone. I don't know what he does
for a living, but Jerry comes with enough
money to get table dances from all of us! As
a matter of fact, I need to give you a table
dance!"

"I'm sorry, Renee, but I didn't know we
were coming here, so I really don't have any
money. Jerry told me to leave it at home."

"Look, Silly, I said I'm going to **give** you
a dance. It's the least I can do for a great
warrior."

As she started to dance for him, he held
back a smile as he thought, *"'Wars don't
make one great.'"* She finished her dance
and returned to the stage.

At different times, the other girls left the
two men to make their appearances on-
stage. Jerry and Eiric talked about old
times in high school and about their new
lives for another hour before Jerry said,

"Come on, Man, let's get outta here. We're gonna go to this club Amber told me about. She's coming after she gets off work, probably with Jamaica. Meanwhile, we can go jam until they show up." Eiric agreed and they left the strip club behind.

A short time later, they went into a club filled with the same smell of cigarette smoke and beer, but no stripper poles. Jerry said this was his first time here and needed to find a restroom. They decided to meet at the bar later as Eiric made his way to the dance floor. He danced with several women for what seemed like hours. He was drenched with sweat so he reached into his pocket to pull out his handkerchief, but instead retrieved a napkin with a phone number. It was Renee's. He left the dance floor to find his friend.

After drying himself in the men's room, he looked towards the bar. After scanning the area a few seconds, he spotted Jerry at a small table with a very pretty lady who stared intensely as he spoke to her. *Cat Daddy! That's what Big Greasy would say. My boy is pulling women left and right! And this one, he doesn't have to pay for!* He laughed as he walked to the table. He wasn't going to interrupt them. He was simply going closer so his friend would see him.

As he got closer, he heard Jerry speaking loudly over the music. "...I'm just glad I didn't shoot them! I mean, one of them was an old man, probably somebody's grandpa. The other guy I almost shot was just a kid, a teenager. I could see the fear in their eyes as I looked at them. I mean, I could have killed both of them, but I spared them. In a war, you can kill for your country, for all you people back home, but I decided not to be a murderer."

"Wutdafuck!" Eiric yelled.

"Hey, Eiric! Cindy, this is my buddy, Eiric, I was telling you about. He was over there, too." Jerry raised his eyebrows at Eiric after the girl turned to look at him. "I was just telling her about all the horrors over there."

"Man, I can't believe you! You're using my stories to get with some chick? How sorry is that? Man, I can't believe you, you fuckin' civilian!" He struggled to control the rage building inside him. Jerry was his friend, somebody he thought he could trust. He hadn't even told Gandhi all the things he told Jerry about the war. Hearing his words being twisted into cheap pick-up lines quickened his heartbeat and respirations. His eyes narrowed into tiny slits, only able to see targets. His forearms tensed and relaxed as his fingertips pressed into his palms, forming tight knots.

A picture of him pounding Jerry's head repeatedly with his fists developed in his mind. Eiric shook his head as another image, one of Jerry's skull breaking open like a piñata, spilling out brains instead of candy, replaced the first.

"Look, my Nigga, I think you forget who you're talking too!" Jerry said indignantly.

"What did you say?" Eiric asked in a surprisingly calm tone.

"You don't know who you're talking too! I'm the one that brought you here!" *Hell, I took you to meet my girl, and you got a lap dance, because of me! I don't see any of your black friends taking you out and hooking you up! If it wasn't for me, your bitch-ass would still be sitting at your mama's house, shell-shocked!*

"No, I mean before that. What did you call me?"

"What?" Jerry smirked. "I can't call you my Nigg..." A blinding-fast right jab to his mouth finished Jerry's sentence. The girl slid away from the table and disappeared into the crowd. People stopped drinking and socializing to look at the bloody scene. Eiric was standing over his old friend poised to strike again. He didn't know which hurt more, the betrayal of his trust, the unexpected racial slur, or the knuckle he cut when he hit Jerry. He relaxed his stance and extended his hand as Jerry struggled to get off the floor. Jerry knocked his hand away.

"Get away from me! I take you out and try to show you a good time and this is the gratitude I get? I take it back, you're not **my Nigga**! You're just **a nigger**! A coward of a nigger that can't kill his enemies but has no problem taking a cheap shot at somebody who tried to be a friend! Fuck you, you Oreo!"

Eiric resisted the urge to hit his former friend any more. He simply turned away and left the club. It was a long walk home, but it didn't matter. He realized that tonight he had travelled a lot farther, going from best friend to nigger in just a few seconds.

County EMS

Monday morning came and Eiric arrived for work 15 minutes early. At every reflective surface, he checked out his uniform. He wanted everything to be perfect on his first day. As he marched through the halls of the station, he tuned in to the laughter and loud talk coming from a brightly lit room at the end of the corridor. *That must be the break room,* he thought as he got closer. He had been instructed to meet there and wait for his orientation partner. He took a deep breath and put a smile on his face as he entered the room.

Several men and women, some seated, some standing around a large, round table, looked towards him as he entered the room. Some nodded at him, one waved, as they continued their conversations. Eiric took an empty seat next to two people who weren't talking. They looked nervous so he assumed they were also new. He said hello and they politely returned his greeting and fell silent again. The others in the break room were drinking coffee and sodas while talking about everything from NASCAR to the weekend arrest report in the local paper.

Some were giving their accounts of a car wreck that had happened Saturday night involving a small car, a wild turkey, and a tree. A young man was driving on a back road headed home from a date when a wild turkey flew out, crashing into the front of his car. He slammed on the brakes, swerved, and the passenger's tail end struck a tree. The car was totaled and the man broke his nose in the crash. The turkey, even though pretty good-sized, never had a chance and was found dead on arrival. The splattered bird was barely recognizable, a matter of considerable disappointment for at least one volunteer fireman on scene who had hoped to make a meal out of the deceased, or at least a trophy to mount on his wall. Apparently, this particular fireman was well-known for his affinity for eating road kill.

Minutes later, another woman came into the room. Her face showed signs of nerves but her voice was confidant as she yelled,

"Hey, Y'all! I'm here! Give me the keys to a truck so we can hit the road!" The woman's entrance broke up the conversations as each person said hello to her. She gave hugs to the old timer's and Eiric learned a few things about her as she made her way around the room.

Her name was Jasmine, or Jazz, and she was a bartender at a small club outside town. She had recently finished her EMT training where most of the paramedics present had been her instructors. She seemed to be well-liked, and a few of the men expressed their hopes that she would be teaming up with them, on the ambulance, of course. After speaking to the paramedics, she came over to the quiet people near Eiric.

"Hey, Kenny! Hey, Marge! Haven't seen y'all since class." The three of them had been in the same EMT course, but only one, Jazz, had made a lasting impression on the paramedics. She talked a few minutes with Kenny and Marge and then pulled up a chair and introduced herself to Eiric. "Hey! I don't think I know you, my name is

Jasmine, but everybody calls me Jazz!" Eiric
shook hands and tried to introduce himself.
He couldn't give more than his first name
since the Shift Supervisor came in and
placed the crew assignments on the board
at the back of the room. Eiric approached
one of the training officers, Robbie, to
comment about his assignment.

"Mr. Daniels, I thought you guys said in
my interview that I would be primarily on
the emergency ACLS trucks? I see that you
partnered me with Jazz on the Convalescent
truck."

Robbie moved in, too close, to Eiric and
began to speak in a deliberately slow
whisper. "Yeah, um, you see, um, we put
you on the slow truck 'cause you already
have so much more experience than the
other EMTs." *You uppity nigger!* "Yeah,
we're gonna get you on the emergency
trucks," *When pigs fly!* "It's just that, for a
while, we want to put the newbies with
more seasoned medics." *This is just what
we need, a trouble-maker. Why can't you
just be satisfied that we hired you? I knew
this would happen.* "Um, I'm sure you can

teach Jazz a lot. Besides, taking people to their doctor's appointments is real important and some of these patients are real sick. You guys could go with your whoopee lights and sirens on some runs! Let her drive while you take care of the patients in the back of the truck." *Yeah, in the **back of the truck!***

"Once we feel the others are comfortable riding on the emergent runs, we'll swap out the two of you." *Nobody's gonna be comfortable 'til we get rid of your black ass!* Eiric accepted his answer and went out to the ambulance bay where Jazz was checking out their truck.

"Looks like you're stuck with me!" she said cheerily. He opened his mouth to respond but she cut him off. "Come on, we got an 8:15 pickup and I'm ready to get this Baby on the road," she said as she patted the side of their truck. "Who knows, maybe we'll get to see some real action before the day is over." Eiric climbed in on the passenger side and buckled himself in as they pulled out of the garage. He grabbed the mic and read from the list of 10 codes, a list of brief radio talk, to inform Dispatch they were on their way. He tried not to notice as she undid the top two buttons of her shirt exposing her ample cleavage. "It's gonna be a hot one!" she exclaimed, as she turned the AC on full blast.

It's gonna be a long one, he thought. He had already decided he needed to prove he was as good as any other medic in the squad. There was no way he was going to let himself get distracted by a pretty face and a nice body. Robbie had enough faith in him to make him the senior medic on this truck, so he was not going to let him down by flirting with this brand new EMT.

On the way to their first appointment, Jazz talked about how she had always dreamed of driving an ambulance. Eiric nodded as he listened to her talk about her dreams of saving lives and finally getting respect from people in the county. She seemed really nice but being nice could get a pretty girl with an outgoing personality, and a banging body, the wrong reputation. They picked up their first patient and delivered her safely to her appointment for dialysis. She would need to be returned home in about 4 hours, so that gave them plenty of time to squeeze in a few more transports.

As they turned to leave the clinic, they heard a woman yell, "Eiric!" They spun around and saw a beautiful woman running up to Eiric.

"Hey, S-S-Sheila!" he stuttered. Sheila Dupare was a classmate from high school. She also happened to be one of Eiric's biggest crushes. She ran up to him and gave him a friendly hug.

"I heard you were home and you were gonna be working for EMS! I saw you when you came in but I was busy with one of my patients! It's good to see you! You didn't get hurt over there, did you?" Her face was pained as she examined him head to toe. He shook his head and opened his mouth to speak but she cut him off. "You didn't kill anybody, did you? What am I saying, of course you didn't! You wouldn't hurt a fly! I'm sorry I asked you that, I guess I'm nervous. I'm just glad to see you're okay!"

Jazz took the stretcher to the truck while they finished talking. "Eiric, be careful with those EMS people," Sheila warned, looking at his partner.

"They're alright."

"Listen. Come back and see me when you're off. You can fill out an application. We're gonna be hiring soon, and it never hurts to have a plan B. I'm just saying, you can't be too careful. Besides, all those heffahs in here are going crazy over you!"

Eiric promised he would and then watched her as she returned to the treatment area. Even if he didn't make it back to the clinic after work, he knew that he would see her tonight, just like he had so many nights before in high school...in his dreams! He joined his partner at the truck and they drove off to transport more patients to their appointments.

"I'm gonna have to get used to this! I'm usually the center of attention! All the ladies in there were checking you out! That last one that chased you outside sure was pretty," Jazz stated as they left the clinic. "Is she one of your girlfriends?"

"She's just a friend, that's all."

"Okay, 'Just a friend!'" Jazz laughed. "But she's still fine! I didn't hear you stutter when you talked to the other females and none of them chased you outside to hug you!"

They made their way to several other patients going to various doctor's offices and clinics before returning to the dialysis clinic. As they arrived at each place, they were met by people with wide eyes and open mouths. They men smiled at Jazz and seemed in a trance, unconsciously following her every move. Her uniform clung tightly against her frame and each breath she took seemed to enlarge her breasts. Her utility belt danced on her waist, her hips rolling gently as she walked with perfect posture. She exaggerated every movement and smiled coyly as the men helped her with the stretcher. The men also watched Eiric closely, hating and envying him immediately.

The women at each facility gave Eiric plenty of attention as well. He was pulled to the side repeatedly by black nurses and aides, shocked to see a black EMT. Over and over, they expressed disbelief and praise as he attempted to remain professional gathering patients' information. A few handwritten phone numbers were attached to typed demographic sheets. Eiric kept his tone flat as he overlooked batting eyelashes and tried to tune out honey-dripped voices from the over-worked, apparently under-sexed women, flirting with him. They displayed more inappropriate behavior than the men lusting over Jazz, slowly licking their lips, openly admiring his visible chest hair, or pinching his butt.

Eventually, they returned to the dialysis clinic, and Eiric and Sheila exchanged numbers before he and Jazz placed their patient on the stretcher. After returning her home, they stopped for lunch at a diner. Eiric had never gone inside this place but knew it well. Because they offered special discounts to County employees that may not be able to finish their meals because of 911 calls, it was the preferred eating establishment of law enforcement, fire, and EMS.

He heard the food was good, but Eiric had never seen any Blacks eating there. None of his family ever mentioned eating at this place. He was nervous as they entered the building. They each noticed the attention they were attracting. Eiric lifted his radio and called in their position to the dispatcher. Several men were mumbling to each other as they shook their heads. Jazz led the way to the counter and they placed their orders. All eyes in the diner watched their every move as they took their trays to a corner table. A few patrons left their meals and exited the diner as the two sat down together.

Jazz ignored the people around them and continued getting to know her partner. Eiric was unaware that he was continuously scanning the room, homing in on any abrupt movement. He always felt uncomfortable talking to strangers about his experience in the war, but this time, with all the staring eyes on him, he actually felt fear. When he mentioned the war, Jazz slammed her palm on the table and shouted, "That's right! I almost forgot!" Eiric braced himself for the question everybody asked. "Did you have to take care of a lot of injured soldiers?"

Eiric was shocked. *What, she didn't ask if I killed anybody?* He answered her politely, not going into detail about the wounds he treated. She was intense as she dug deeper making him tell her everything. She seemed to get a rush out of hearing him talk about traumatic scenes. She was very animated as she plied him for more details about grisly scenarios.

He smiled in between bites of food, which was really good, and gave her a breakdown of the types of wounds he had treated. He thought it would be difficult talking about his experience but Jazz made him feel at ease. She was able to craft her questions to focus on the treatment of the wounds and what they looked like while avoiding the subject of where the events took place. He didn't feel like he was talking about a war. With Jazz, he felt he was just talking about a normal day at work.

She eventually changed the subject. "You know, working with you is like hanging out with a celebrity." He raised an eyebrow as he swallowed his food. "Come, on, everywhere we go, the ladies are all over you. You get hit on more than I do, and that says a lot! But, you just act all cool and professional. I guess you're just used to all the attention. Either that or you're gay. I don't mean any harm, and it doesn't matter to me, but these women were going crazy over you and you just blew them off."

He laughed. "Well, I'm not gay! I really don't know what you're talking about. I was just giving reports to the nurses, doing my job, nothing more. I don't think anybody was hitting on me." *Well, maybe the lady who grabbed my butt or hopefully, Sheila!*

"You're probably right, nobody was hitting on you. Especially not that sexy one, Sheila. I don't think you're her type." Eiric's eyebrows jumped towards his scalp before settling back in place. "The one lady that pinched your booty though, was definitely flirting with you. Yeah, I saw her! I wonder what you would do if somebody really came on strong." She leaned closer to the table and slowly whispered, "You know, you have the longest, prettiest eyelashes I've ever seen on a man." With every word, her breasts screamed for attention.

Eiric avoided temptation by looking around the diner. He may not have given her the reaction she was looking for, but the others were fully engulfed with the scene at their table. He turned back to his partner and met her gaze. She grinned and toyed with the straw in her cup. They finished their meal and returned to their ambulance, still scanned by every eye in the place.

In the privacy of the cab, Jazz's smile disappeared. "Fucking hicks! I can't stand them! I don't know which ones burn me up more, the retards staring at us the whole time or the assholes that got up and left because we sat down to eat together! One day, I'm getting out of this small town and away from these simple-minded rednecks!"

"Calm down, Jazz. You can't get yourself all worked up because of them. It's probably the first time they ever saw medics like us. You know, the kind that might actually know what a gym is!" They both laughed. It was true that most of the paramedics had trouble squeezing into their XXL uniforms.

"I don't know how you can just take that kind of shit!" she complained. I guess you just get used to it, but it would drive me crazy! You know something, I like you. All day yesterday, when I was getting ready for this, I wondered how the day was gonna go on the truck with you. You're different from what I expected, though."

"What do you mean by that? How could you expect anything from me when we just met today?" Eiric asked.

"You're right, we just met, but I knew all about you long before I came into the squad room this morning. I trust you, Eiric. All day long, you've looked me in the eyes when we talked." She buttoned her blouse to properly cover herself and continued. "I'm sorry I tried to set you up with My

Girls. Our new bosses wanted you to make a pass or say something inappropriate to me so they could fire you for sexual harassment. They told me Friday, that you were gonna be my partner and what they wanted me to do."

She watched the confusion settle on his face before going on. "You do know why they hired us, don't you? They hired me because everyone thinks I'm a whore. That's cool, I don't care what they think, as long as they pay me and let me ride the emergency calls once in a while. They all think it will be easy to get in my pants as soon as we're alone on one of these trucks. Wrong answer! Everybody knows, male and female crews hook up. They work 24-hour shifts, eating and sleeping together, so it's bound to happen, even if they're married. Horny perverts!

"Eiric, you seem like a nice guy and I know you're a good medic, but they only hired you to keep from getting sued by the N, double-A, C, P. You might not know this because it happened before you came home, but a few months back, there was a lot in the news about there wasn't enough minorities being represented in the county. They had some legit complaints, like, there aren't that many black cops, firemen, or elected officials and, until you, no minority medics working for EMS.

"Then, they started talking about getting rid of the monument. White people were kind of listening to them until they started in on that damn statue! You would think it was a real person! There were all kinds of protests on both sides. Nobody got hurt but a lot of people were pissed off. Still are. Anyway, black people knew they weren't going to be able to do anything about the Confederate statue but they knew they could hurt the county with a law suit.

"Then, you came home. You made the paper, a black war hero! Everybody knows you, they know you were an Army medic, so they couldn't wait for you to apply. Somebody they could hire to shut up the Blacks and then fire as soon as you did something wrong, like try to screw the local slut they hired."

Eiric absorbed her words and let his temper simmer on low. He smiled at her but in his head other thoughts formed. *Ok, so I don't go crazy over your breasts, so you come up with this crap. Maybe they hired you 'cause you are a ho, I don't know. Me, they hired 'cause they needed at least one EMT who actually knows what he's doing. Still, you're nice and you mean well. I'll teach you what I know so maybe you'll get their respect. Robbie's counting on me to help out with you and the other rookies and I don't plan on letting him down.*

"Look, I can't just go in and get a job based on my good looks. I have to rely on my skills. I don't believe I was hired for any other reason."

"Hmm, well I can't just go in and get a job based on my skills! I have to rely on my good looks!" They both laughed. "Seriously, I know they only hired my boobies! But I know something they don't. Those idiots messed around and hired two minorities! Those stupid horn-dogs, drooling at the chance to screw me, will never know that they're not my type." She paused and nodded at Eiric.

"Oh...you like Brothers?" he stammered.

"Yes, I like Brothers, but that's not what I mean. I like soft, beautiful things." Eiric looked puzzled. She cocked her head to the side and said, "Females, Eiric!"

"Oh...okay! That's cool!" He didn't know what else to say. "So, what are you going to say to them about me, since I didn't hit on you?"

"I'll tell them the truth. I put My Girls all up in your face but you didn't even glance at them! Did you?" A sly look crossed his face as he arched his eyebrows. She grinned. *Yeah, he looked!* "Eiric, you nasty boy! And here I was, thinking I lost my touch because you didn't make it obvious. Why, if I wasn't a lesbian, I'd rock your world! Still, you're kind-a cute and all these women keep creaming over you. They might know something I don't. I can imagine their faces back at the station. I might give you some just to piss them off! Don't worry about what I'm gonna say to them. You have more ammunition to get me fired than I have against you." He frowned at her. "If you think these bigots hate Blacks, how do you think they feel about homosexuals?"

They continued to work, transporting people to different doctor's appointments but they kept the rest of their conversations mostly on business. At the end of their day, they were met by lots of grinning faces at the station. Eiric was allowed to leave but Jazz was called to the office to 'complete some paperwork.' She looked at Eiric with the same grin she had when they were alone in the truck earlier. He nodded at her as she disappeared into the main office and then he left for home.

On his way home, he took a detour. *I've always wanted to do this.* He made a turn to the Volunteer Rescue Station to sign up. He slowly pulled into the parking lot, filled with pick-up trucks. *Man, this place is packed. Hope they're taking applications. These guys see just as much action as the County, only, they do it for free.*

He parked his car and went inside the office, still in his EMS uniform. Inside, there were four men, three white and one black, seated behind desks. Eiric went to the man at the largest desk and introduced himself. "I work for the County EMS, but I also want to join you guys and work on my off days."

Behind him a voice joked, "Hell, now we can put a sign on the roof that says, 'Watermelon and fried chicken every Tuesday night!'" Eiric spun around and saw the men behind him rolling with laughter. The black man at the corner desk, also laughing, looked up from his typewriter at Eiric and urged him to join in the fun. Eiric stared stone-faced at this man before turning back to the man in charge, who handed him an application. Eiric was quiet as he quickly made his exit. When the door closed, he heard the same voice yell something about a, "Super nigger!"

As he got in his car, he noticed all the gun racks and rebel flags in the parked trucks. He ripped the paper to shreds and drove away. The next few weeks, Eiric found himself partnered with Jazz or the other new EMTs, still on the convalescent truck. The other EMTs, all inexperienced, had picked up several days on the ACLS trucks, responding to emergency calls.

One of the paramedics, Aaron, seemed to support Eiric's bid to ride the emergency trucks one day. "We need to put him on one of the A-Trucks! Shoot, it's almost the first of the month, and you know what that means...they'll be going crazy over in the hood! We can go into the projects, now that we have Eiric!"

Eiric stored this away as just another bad joke, but he remembered all the times he had watched paramedics dawdle, drinking coffee and talking after being dispatched to Black or Hispanic neighborhoods. They knew they had a minimum response time of three minutes to answer a call and get underway and they never failed to wait every second before responding to one of these calls. It made Eiric remember Gandhi once talking about slow 911 calls. *The only time 911 comes fast, is to arrest your black ass!*

When he was finally assigned to ride an ACLS ambulance, he was surprised to see who his partner was. Earl, the shopkeeper, came up to him, in an EMS uniform, and said, "All rat, let's get goin'." Besides being a tailor, Earl was one of the training officers for the County. He sat in silence, only speaking to give Eiric directions as they drove around.

Before noon, they were dispatched to an emergency in a neighborhood Eiric knew well. His family had lived there for years before moving to the country. Some kid on a bike had been hit by a car. He and Earl arrived within minutes of the call, sirens blazing. A crowd of people gathered around the boy on the ground. He recognized some of them as friends of his family, but they all looked at Eiric like he was a creature returned from the grave. *Damn, when he said they would look at me this way, I assumed he meant white people.* He asked if anybody knew the boy's name but no one answered. *Nobody knows him?*

He gently stabilized the boy's head and neck while Earl checked him over. Eiric then gave directions to the crowd to move back and secure the bicycle. Nobody moved until Earl said the same thing. *What the hell? He just said the same thing I did, word for word.* Eiric and Earl began treating the boy's wounds and they were joined some time later by the volunteer rescue squad. They assisted with placing him on a stretcher and loading him in the back of the truck where Earl started an IV. Eiric closed the doors and one of the volunteers asked why he hadn't returned with his application. Eiric recognized the man and answered him dryly, "I don't like watermelon and fried chicken."

He then asked the injured boy's mother to join him in the cab of the ambulance. He must have been speaking a foreign language because the woman didn't move until the volunteer fireman told her to get in the ambulance. *I can't remember her name, but his woman has known my family forever! Now she can't accept a simple request from me? Mr. Joker shows up, tells her to do the exact same thing I said, and she jumps in the truck! Was I speaking German?*

He shook his head as he climbed into Squad 3. Eiric turned on the siren and drove to the ER where the boy was quickly taken to the back to be seen by the doctor. As Eiric cleaned the stretcher, a tall, black man, one of the ER nurses, asked him to come into their break room. Eiric followed and the nurse shook his hand as soon as the door closed.

"My name's Trey, I'm one of the triage nurses here. Man, you're the first black EMT they've ever had!"

Oh, no, another Gandhi, Eiric thought. *I wonder what he's about to say about 'The Man.'*

"I'm the first black male nurse to graduate from the local college, so that puts us in a very exclusive club, Brother! If you ever need anything, or these Rednecks give you any trouble, let me know." He handed Eiric a business card.

Great, Eiric thought as he examined the card. *I bet Gandhi would love this. Dude, they hired me because I'm qualified.* "Thanks, but I don't want to join the NAACP, or any other group. They're treating me fair, and that's all I asked for."

"Ok, Brother, if you say so. Just keep your eyes open and watch your back. If they're treating you fair, you must be a different kind of Brother!"

They returned to the lobby and found Earl finishing the stretcher. He eyeballed Trey as he called out, "What's up, Earl?" before returning to his desk. Eiric noticed that Earl had a disgusted look on his face as he turned from Trey without answering. Earl walked away to the ambulance and Eiric followed with the stretcher. Once again, they rode in silence except for Earl giving occasional directions to turn here or there.

After a long while of driving in the country, Earl directed Eiric to pull over by a pasture enclosed by a barbed-wire fence. When they stopped, Earl spoke to the younger man.

"I liked how you handled yourself on that call today. You did everythang rat. You see this road?" Earl pointed to a dirt road that parted the pasture and led into a stand of tall trees. Eiric nodded.

"Ok. Well, from time to time, especially in the summer, we get calls out here. This is a Klan training camp. In the summer, they have kids out here and sometimes somebody gets a broken arm, leg, or somethin' they can't handle on their own. If you're ridin' with me and we get a call out here, I'm gonna let you out rat here and then pick you up on my way back out. I can't guarantee your safety inside their compound. They won't like havin' a black person in there, even if you're comin' to help.

"If you're ridin' with somebody else and y'all get a call to come here, you tell whoever your partner is to let you out. I don't care if they threaten to fire you or even if they don't stop the truck, you get the hell out and wait up here! When they come out, if they don't stop to let you back in, go back down to the intersection and call me from that gas station. I'll come and get you, but you'll probably want to hide until you see my truck. You understand what I'm sayin'?" Eiric nodded. "Ok, let's get on back to the station." He saw Eiric's nostrils flaring. "What's wrong?"

"Man, I've been past this place all my life and never knew the KKK was in there."

"And if anybody asks, you still don't! The Klan ain't goin' nowhere, they thrive on secrecy. You're not the only one that could get hurt if they found out I told you. And another thang, I can't tell you who to be friends with, but that nurse, Trey, is somebody you might wanna distance yourself from. He can't keep his mouth shut and there's plenty a folks 'round here that want to shut it for him! Same thang goes for your family."

"Are you threatening my family?"

"Naw, I ain't threatenin' nobody! I'm tryin' to tell you some thangs to keep you and your'n safe! I told you before, people don't like how your folks bought that property in the country. They call 'em 'uppity.' Now, here you are, riding in the county's ambulances. They know your parents, your grandparents, aunts, uncles, cousins and where they all live. They might not hurt them directly but you know they can be left hanging for EMS response. That includes police and fire, too. Be careful's all I'm sayin'."

They rode back to the station without any further conversation. Eiric tried to process what he had heard and seen this day. *I still have to work all night with this dude. I wonder what else he's gonna reveal to 'help me out.' I don't care what he or anybody else says, I'm gonna prove myself just like I did in the Army. Am I the only person in this county that's not a racist? I don't remember things being this bad before I went to the Army. It doesn't matter. I'll just keep being me and one day they'll have to accept me for who I am.*

They didn't receive any more calls that night. Earl advised him to get some rest, but Eiric wasn't able to sleep. Instead, he pulled his mustang into the back of the ambulance bay and did a thorough detailing of the car. The next morning, Earl came into the bay and was amazed at how clean the car was. "Damn, Son, you stayed up all night cleanin' her?" Eiric nodded. "You did a good job! It looks like a pitcher in a magazine!"

"Thanks, Earl. I used to clean cars in high school with a buddy of mine. We made pretty good money, more than I would pay to have somebody else clean my car." Earl sipped his coffee as he continued to walk around the car. Eiric popped the hood and the trunk to show off how clean they were.

"You cleaned the engine and the trunk, too? That's a work of art!" he said, as he extended his right hand to Eiric. They shook hands and grinned at the gleaming vehicle before them. Pretty soon, the voices of the medics coming in to work drifted into the bay. Some came into garage and when they saw the mustang, the commotion they made attracted all the others. Earl eagerly repeated the same thing, as each new group of medics came into the bay.

"He stayed up all night and cleaned this baby! Just look at her!" The others joined in, complementing the spotless car, wishing their own looked half as good.

Eiric was proud of his work but even more than that, he felt like he was part of the team. *I should have cleaned my car a long time ago.* He decided to help out the crew relieving him and Earl by completing the ambulance inspection for them. The others continued to talk as he slipped to the front of the bay to the cab of Squad 3. He worked silently, wanting to surprise his relief. He had just finished checking out the oxygen tanks when he heard something that caught his attention.

"You know, I didn't think he was a real nigger until I saw this shiny car! You know how they keep their rides clean!" The voice belonged to Aaron, one of the paramedics assigned to Squad 3 today.

Another paramedic, Jenny, added, "Yeah, them niggers will put $10,000 worth of tires and stereos on a $2,000 car while they live in a $500 apartment! And all of it paid for by us taxpayers! Niggers and wet-backs can't wait to spend up them gov'ment checks! How much y'all wanna bet he's paying for this car with **our** tax money?"

Someone else provided another theory. "Y'all know that boy can't afford this kinda car off what he's makin' here. I thank it's safe to say, he's slangin' dope! Typical nigger shit! Hell, I betcha he's tryin' to steal summa the meds off the trucks to sell on the streets. Them dumbass niggers will shoot up or smoke just about anythang! It won't be long before we find out he's a gangbanger, betcha!" This sounded like Karen.

"Shit, what do you think he was doin' in the military? That's where bangers go to get more training! They practice on each other in the streets with their drive-by's! Then, they go in the military and they come out, knowin' how to kill even better! They learn how to **aim**, and use plastic explosives, and make 'in-provised' weapons. The Army and Marines is full-a nuthin' but niggers doin' nuthin' but learnin' how to kill us!" Willie James stated.

Eiric was furious as he put faces to the voices. Other people had similar things to say about Eiric, Blacks, and Hispanics. Only one person spoke kindly of Eiric.

Earl's voice was heard asking, "What? I can't believe y'all! That young man is a decorated war hero! We didn't go on any runs last night, so he used his time wisely, and all y'all kin do is trash talk?"

"Fuck you, Earl! Get the hell outta here and go on back to your shop! I swear, you're a step away from joinin' the fuckin' N-fuckin'-C-A-P-fuckin' double-A, you fuckin' nigger lover!" screamed Willie James.

Eiric's first impulse was to run into the middle of these paramedics, cuss them out, hit a few, and quit his job. Instead, he quietly slipped out of the bay through a side door. He walked to the rear entrance to the bay and opened the door to join the crowd around his car. He put on a sad face and did his best to look worn out as he slowly walked towards them.

"Hey, y'all, look! Here comes Eiric, now!" It was Aaron speaking. "We was all just talkin' 'bout the damn good job you did on this here Boss! Man, she shore is purty!"

"It's just a car," Eiric replied.

"Shoot, I bet your house is not this clean?" Jenny said with a huge smile.

"Well, you would lose that bet. I live at home with my parents and my mom keeps her house spotless. I don't clean my car that often, for two reasons. One, my fingers get cold easily ever since I got a cold-weather injury in Germany. Second, I usually don't have time to clean my car, between working here, trying to go to nursing school, and then reporting for duty in the Reserves once a month. I got it this clean because I might have to sell it. Don't know if I can afford it. Maybe y'all can give me a raise?"

Aaron spoke up. "I know you're making all the money in the military! Plus, all the benefits y'all get."

"Everybody has their own reason for joining but getting rich is not one of them. We don't really make a lot. For all we do to protect the country, we get pennies. I joined for the college money, and it doesn't cover everything. I did learn a lot in the Army that's helping me in school and with working with civilians."

Willie James joked, "Yeah, how to shoot and blow shit up! We know how y'all are!" The others laughed nervously, giving him stern looks.

Eiric's voice was soft as he responded, "Yes, I did learn all that. I'm pretty good, if I say so, myself." His eyes burned into Willie's. "I also learned that I really love this country and I would die protecting all of you from our enemies. Of course, I would rather make my enemies die for their country." Everybody seemed to like his answer, congratulating him as they made their way out of the garage.

Only Earl remained behind with a hard look on his face. "Eiric, you ever hear about the bird that didn't fly south for winter?" He shook his head and Earl continued.

"Well, one day he gets real cold as he's walkin' in a pasture. He sees this cow, so he gets closer to get warm. Now, the cow plops a big one, rat on top-a him. The bird starts screamin' his head off and this cat walkin' by hears him inside the pile of manure. The cat digs him out, the bird smiles, and the cat smiles back at him. Then, the cat eats the bird. The moral of the story is, 'Everybody who smiles at you is not your friend. Everybody that shits on you is not your enemy. Even if you're in deep doo-doo, as long as you're safe and warm, keep your mouth shut.'" Earl waited a second before stating, "Be careful who you make friends with."

Eiric shook the older man's hand and said, "I always do. Thank you, Mr. Earl." After punching out, Eiric drove slowly out of the garage into the bright morning light. When he got to the highway, he floored the gas pedal and the engine responded with a deep-throated roar, as it rocketed over the asphalt towards home. For several miles, he did 120 in a 55-mph zone. Recognizing familiar landmarks, he slowed down to the legal limit as he neared the driveway to his family's home.

He parked his car at the top of the drive as tears slid from his eyes. He clenched his fists in an attempt to subdue the tremors that began to rock his body. Though the AC was on high, his uniform was soaked in sweat. He shook his head forcefully to rid his brain of evil thoughts about his co-workers.

He succeeded in getting the faces of the paramedics out of his mind. They, however, were quickly replaced by demolished buildings, charred military vehicles, and bloody people. The music from his stereo was drowned out by artillery explosions, whistling bullets, and grown men crying like babies. As he crossed his arms close to his chest, an eerie wail issued from his lungs, but he was only aware of the sounds and sights in his head.

He was forced to revisit scenes he wished he had never laid eyes on. Random body parts covered in blood and soot dotted the sand. Amputees, in varying stages of shock, shuffled around like zombies, searching for their missing parts. He saw bodies torn in half, people holding their own organs on display, like demented butchers, proud of their goods. He saw children playing a game of hop-scotch over landmines, some winning, but far too many losing. A young girl and her little brother, he assumed, reached out bandaged hands to accept chocolate from the American soldiers, partly responsible for the destruction of their village. He saw the faces of people he didn't know but would never forget. His friend, Big O, lay stretched out in an expanding pool of his own blood, reaching out for help as Eiric stood paralyzed. He viewed his own hand clutching the handle of his bayonet while he kneeled next to a wounded Iraqi Republican Guard.

Suddenly, Eiric felt the cold, rushing air through his wet shirt and heard the guitar rift from his radio and realized where he really was and what had just happened to him. He had slipped away into another dreamscape, reliving moments he could not erase, no matter how hard he tried to forget. The same song that was playing when he turned into the drive was just ending. Confused, he shook his head trying to figure out just how long he had been parked here. What had taken only minutes, seemed like days. A dreadful feeling of helplessness and fear overcame him.

Wow, this happened while I was parked here at home, but what if I blacked out while I was driving or taking care of a patient? I can't live like this! That seemed so real! Big O, all shot up and I froze! That pretty little girl with the limp, 'Monkey Foot,' and her little brother, 'Toothless,' coming back for candy after I wrapped up their wounds. All those other people, women and little kids, burned, cut, and shot the hell up! And what was I doing with that knife in my hand?

He got out of his car and opened the trunk. He quickly found the items he was looking for and returned to his seat behind the wheel. He had been told several times about his screaming in the night that he was unaware of. He even realized there had been moments when he couldn't remember how he had gotten to a particular place or why time had passed without his noticing. This time, he could remember what he had seen in his trance.

That's why people are afraid of me. They can see where I've been, what I've done! I can't take this shit! Why did I even go in the Army? Oh, yeah, money for school! I went to a fucking war just to get a few dollars for a school I can't even get into! But everybody wants to thank me for what I did over there. What did I do? All those Iraqis, dead, dying, or hurt just from being in the wrong place at the wrong time. Even the soldiers didn't want to be fighting against us! That didn't stop them from shooting at us, though. I let Big O just lay there bleeding while I punked

*out! I wanted to leave the Scouts, MY
FRIENDS, when they needed me the most.
Everybody keeps calling me a hero, but I
know what I am. A coward! I should have
been the one bleeding in the sand! I'm so
sorry, O!*

Eiric tightly gripped the items he had
retrieved from his trunk. He pulled back on
the slide of the pistol after inserting the
loaded magazine. Tears mixed with sweat
as he placed the end of the barrel against
his temple. He looked into the rear-view
mirror and stared into his own eyes. He
willed the tears to stop by reciting the verse
he had used in the Gulf. "Can't see through
tears. Can't see through tears." He felt
extremely calm, relaxed, except for the
hand holding the gun.

As his trigger finger began to tense, the
sound of a lawn mower filtered through his
closed window. He straightened his finger
and turned his head slightly to the left. He
saw one of their neighbors, Mrs. Steiner,
pushing the mower with some effort.
Where's Mr. Steiner, he thought. *She's
killing herself out here while he's inside*

chillin'. This thought made him look at his right hand. The gun was still waiting patiently for him to do something.

He looked at the elderly woman struggling with the machine in a hard-fought battle with unwanted weeds. He turned away from her and looked at his parents' lawn. He thought about all the times he had pushed their lawn mower back and forth, up and down the yard. He remembered small rocks pelting against his jeans or stinging his bare skin. He smiled as he saw himself being chased by yellow jackets one summer after running over their underground nest. Fortunately, he had been able to outrun the bees and get inside the house. He thought about all the times he had to go back and cut the yard again because he had done a crappy job the first time.

A strange sound, half laughter, half crying, burst forth from his lungs. Still holding the weapon, he pounded the heels of his hands against his head until he stopped crying. He dropped the magazine from the pistol and ejected the chambered round onto the passenger seat. He wiped his face and practiced smiling in the mirror. He left his car and crossed his neighbor's lawn, waving at the older woman. Mrs. Steiner protested, but eventually allowed Eiric to finish her lawn.

Gandhi

Eiric tried hard to forget about the events that led up to him mowing the Steiner's lawn weeks ago. Eiric really didn't mind doing the yard for **Mr**. Steiner. He was a popular teacher at his sister's school and always had a huge smile on his face or a joke to share.

Mrs. Steiner, however, was a hard person to like. She never responded when any of his family spoke in passing. In fact, she would either turn her back or pretend not to see them. Eiric's father called her a, "Mean, old bigot," but it was hard for Eiric to write her off as a racist. She always had a sour look on her face, even when she watched her small grandchildren play in her yard. To Eiric, Mrs. Steiner hated everybody equally.

Nothing seemed to give her pleasure, but at odd times she would surprise him. He remembered getting a call from her one day, asking if his mother's dog was home. She was worried because she had just heard squealing brakes as a card skidded to a stop at the top of the driveway. Her voice trembled as she expressed concern for his mother and the possibility of losing her pet.

Eiric felt some remorse at how he had responded to Mrs. Steiner that day. "Yeah, he's right here chewing on a bone. You want to talk to him?" She obviously wasn't fazed by his answer as she simply expressed her relief that the dog was okay. After hanging up the phone, Eiric wondered how this woman could show so much emotion about a dog but look indifferently at people. *Oh, well,* he recalled thinking back then, *I guess dogs are more important than people.*

His mind went back to the day he convinced her to let him finish her yard. *I don't remember her ever asking how I was doing. I've talked with Mr. Steiner several times since I got back, so I guess he reported our conversations to her. Funny, she still hasn't said anything about that day I cut her grass. I know she saw me in the car. She pretends not to, but I know she sees everything.*

Eiric didn't allow himself to dwell on that day. So much had happened since then. He found it hard to work with his co-workers who had talked bad about him when they thought he wasn't around. These same people continued to smile in his face and pat him on the back. He was on-guard, wary of concealed knives, but their hands were empty as they patted him. Or were they *petting* him? Eiric wasn't sure. He quietly did his duties as he kept mental notes of things happening around him.

One day, while he was reading a policy in the break room, he noticed that the room suddenly became uncomfortably silent. The paramedics had just been joking and talking loudly moments before. When Eiric looked up from the manual, all eyes were on him. He looked back at each of them and noticed most of them looked afraid of him. Willie James was beet red as he stared at Eiric, coffee slipping down the side of his Styrofoam cup as his hand trembled. *What's going on? Eiric* wondered.

Suddenly, Willie James dropped his coffee cup in the trash and left the room. The others noisily exhaled and congratulated Eiric on how he had, "Handled the situation."

What situation are they talking about?

One of the paramedics cleared up his confusion. "I thought you were going to bust Willie James in the mouth when he said he hated, uh, you know, the N-word. I hate when people use the N-word, so I know it must really bother you, but you didn't even flinch. I thought for sure you were gonna kill him."

Eiric nodded as he accepted these words from a man who claimed to hate, "the N-word," but frequently talked about, "Niggers." Honestly, Eiric had only, "Handled the situation well," because he was totally unaware that it had occurred. He had been totally absorbed in reading the new policy.

Days later, a paramedic, Lawrence, was reading the newspaper when he abruptly stopped and slammed the folded paper on the table. He rolled his eyes as he turned to

Eiric. "Can you please tell me why bu-lack people hate the Confederate flag so much?"

"Lawrence, I just want to eat my breakfast. I can go somewhere else if I'm bothering you. You might want to ask somebody else that question."

"I'm asking you, because you're the only ni...**Negro**...uh, uh, African-American...uh, uh, I mean, bu-lack person in here."

Eiric considered his words carefully before saying, "I can't answer for all black people. I don't know what black people think any more than what white people, or yellow, or red, or purple people think. I can only speak for myself, and that flag doesn't really concern me. I only care about one flag. Why are you asking me that?"

"They're protesting in South Carolina about taking the flag off their capitol building." Again, Lawrence rolled his eyes, as he began to educate Eiric. "The Confederate flag is a part of history. It's a symbol of States' rights. Bu-lack people think the Civil War was fought over slavery, but it was really fought for State's rights. The federal government wanted to tell

Southern states what they could and couldn't do, just like the British did to the colonies. The South fought for freedom just like the patriots in the Revolutionary War."

"And the Revolutionary patriots got rid of the British flags and gave us a new one. The only one we should be flying. You said, 'The South fought for freedom?' That's what you're trying to tell me? Whose freedom? Man, the South fought for their right to keep slaves. The slaves were not free! You can sit there and try to make yourself feel better about what happened back then, but I can't agree with you."

"That's because your **bu-lack ass leaders** want to rile everybody up by misrepresenting facts! The Civil War was fought so that States could make their **own** laws **for** the people, and **by** the people that lived there, not for slavery! I ain't never had a slave and don't know anybody that has! Why can't y'all just get over it?"

Eiric wanted to remain calm but he raised his voice when he responded, "If the South had won, we wouldn't be having this conversation! Instead of sitting here with you at this table, working **with** you, I would be working **for** you. I would be your property, your **slave**. The South fought the Civil War for their right to keep black people as slaves and that's a fact! Instead of asking me why **some** Blacks hate that damn flag, you might want to ask yourself why **some** white people love it so much!" Eiric left the break room without waiting for an answer.

Days later, during the last hour of his shift, a call had come in from some police requesting EMS a few blocks away. Eiric grabbed an aid bag and said he would respond on-foot since it was so close. He could be there before they rolled an ambulance and would call back if it was needed. When he arrived at the scene, he found two white cops blocking the path of a homeless black man. They were laughing at the man, one getting close up in his face, asking him, "Do-do-do you-you-you want a dr-dr-dr-drink?"

Eiric quietly walked past the officers and placed his bag on the ground beside the man. The police continued laughing as they informed him not to waste his time on this wino. "He's just trying to get a free ride to the ER, so they can give him a sandwich and something to dr-dr-drink!" Eiric gave the officer a cold stare and clenched his jaws. He relaxed his face as he turned towards the homeless man.

The man turned his sad eyes to Eiric and began to speak. "I-I-I-I-I-I'm n-n-n-n-n-not d-d-d-d-drunk, I just st-st-st-st-stutter!" Eiric asked if he could help and the man nodded. Eiric checked his blood sugar as a cop behind him spoke.

"Come on, Tom-Tom-Tom-Tommy! Don't waste this boy's time."

Eiric called for an ambulance to come, as the man's blood sugar was dangerously low. The cops stopped laughing and then wanted to help but Eiric said, "That's okay, you've helped enough." The ambulance arrived and Tommy was helped inside by the two policemen.

Eiric nodded at the man as he looked out at him and said clearly, "Thank you." Something in Tommy's eyes made Eiric feel more self-pride than he had in years. The police tried to apologize for their behavior as the truck went away.

"We thought he was drunk! I didn't know his sugar was low. I hope you're not gonna write this up or anything. We were just having a little fun! I knew something was wrong with him, that's why we called for an ambulance. We're all on the same team, right?" Eiric nodded and gathered his equipment.

Days later, he was called into Robbie's office to talk about his report of the call. Robbie started off with, "I know you meant well by writing every little thing down that you observed on this call, but I can't accept this. There's no way I can let you file this report. It puts those officers in a very bad light and we can't have that. We have to work closely with PD, so we can't go getting those boys in trouble over some bum. I've known Cardwell and Lewis since they were little. They're good boys. You're supposed to write about the patient and what you did to treat him. Instead, you wrote a tirade about what you consider racial injustice. So, I'm gonna give you a few minutes to re-write your report."

"You want me to falsify the report?"

"No, I don't! I want you to report how those police officers stabilized and protected a person with low blood glucose until EMS personnel arrived on-scene. I want you to report the patient's status, care given, and his disposition enroute to the ER. I want you to write an objective **report** and not this subjective **essay**!"

"Everything in that report is an objective observation of what I witnessed that day, Sir! I'm not going to change one word. If those cops look bad, they did it to themselves, Sir."

"I had a feeling you were going to say something like that. Several medics have reported that you're over sensitive. I don't know if you're cut out to work here. EMS workers need to have strong mental discipline. I had my doubts about hiring you from the start, but I was out-voted. I think you might just be proving me right."

He looked over the top of his glasses and down his nose at Eiric. "I'm gonna have to address this matter with the other Supervisors. By the way, I don't need this," he said as he crumpled Eiric's report. "You made up your own special policy when you ran to this scene instead of taking an ambulance. The report filed by the ambulance crew that took Tommy to the ER is the only one I need. Now, you can leave my office!"

Eiric stared at the man across the desk from him, unable to grasp all that had been said. Robbie jumped up slamming both fists on his desk sending papers flying. "I said get the fuck outta my office, you uppity ass ni..." Eiric allowed a smirk to slip on his face as he got up to leave.

The next few weeks were difficult, as Eiric saw his hours were cut drastically. Officially, he was told that everyone's hours were 'under review.' Somehow, he found that hard to believe when he saw that others were actually scheduled to work overtime.

He had a lot of time to spend with himself, which was not always a good thing. Unwanted thoughts found easier access to the front of his head when he was idle. He frequently awoke to find sweat-drenched sheets and worried faces looking at him. He noticed periods of time when he couldn't remember how he had reached a destination or what he had done on the way. All he knew was, he was always covered in sweat and his throat and eyes burned.

He was always tired, irritable, and prone to crying for no apparent reason. He thought about the pain that he would get in his joints at random intervals. It was a debilitating pain that made it difficult to move his arms or even flex his fingers. As suddenly as the pain set in, though, it mysteriously disappeared.

He began to cut his hair shorter and he also forced himself to return to daily shaving. Since becoming a civilian, he had tried to let his beard grow in. He had to give up on this quest, as he noticed circular islands of skin in the midst of a prickly, rough sea of stubble. He would stare at these patches of skin, amazed at their smoothness, as he rubbed the areas. He tried to diagnose the cause, but couldn't, so he simply shaved off everything.

One Sunday morning, his mother came to his room bringing in a new white dress shirt. "I got this for you to wear to church this morning," she said, hanging the shirt next to a black suit she had brought from the cleaners without his knowledge. "Did you call your friend, Gandhi, the other day?"

"Yeah," he lied. With all the problems at his job and the bad dreams he had been having, he wasn't ready to talk with his friend. Somehow, Gandhi would know something was wrong.

"Good!" his mother continued. "He said it was urgent. Now, move it. I gotta get everybody else ready."

"I don't feel like going today. I feel like I didn't sleep at all." He slid his hand over the sheets and was relieved to find them dry. Not since he was very small did he have to worry about wet sheets in the morning.

His mother continued as if he had not said a word. "I fried chicken, and your aunt made a coconut cake for dinner after church. Everybody's bringing a dish for a special dinner after church. Get on up, you don't want to be late."

"Mama, I said, I'm not going! I feel like crap! I'll just get some junk food later or you can bring a plate home. I just can't go this morning."

"You have to go!" Eiric's eyes snapped open. He hadn't been told he had to go to church since he was a little boy. Every Sunday morning back then, he went through the same ritual. He woke up, cleaned himself, and declared he didn't want to go to Sunday school. After a quick, but effective, butt whipping, he would get dressed and wait with the other kids for their grandmother to pick them up to go to church.

"Reverend Marne has something to present to you! Your unit in Germany sent a package here and we wanted to give it to you today, in front of your church family. You have to come! Or do you want a whipping, first?"

"No thank you!" Eiric laughed, as he got out of bed. She left him to get ready for church. He felt guilty as he cleaned up and got dressed. He was ashamed of himself for the way he had acted with his mother.

I should have just said, Yes Ma'am, and got my butt outta bed, especially since she went out of her way to get my clothes for me. What the hell did they send her and why didn't she just give it to me here? She knows I don't like everybody making a fuss over me. I bet they sent one of our 'Raiders of the Enemy' sweaters, since I never bought one. That's why Gandhi called. Oh, well, at least she didn't ask me to wear my uniform. Still, I can't wait to get this over with and get to that chicken! Wait a minute! Is my mama racist 'cause she motivated me with fried chicken? He laughed out loud as he got himself dressed.

Eiric tried every trick he could think of to stay awake during the sermon. He doodled on the back of the program until his mother stopped him. In his head, he recited his general orders and military Code of Conduct. He thought about girls he had known, but quickly asked God for forgiveness. He flexed and relaxed his muscles and even pricked himself with a safety pin he had placed in his pocket to stay awake. He drifted back to thoughts of what this mysterious present might be.

What did that crazy Gandhi send me? I hope it's that picture of all of us at the Cinderella Castle. Or maybe it's one of the company posters we made. Maybe he sent me some Spezi! Man, I love that stuff! I didn't realize how much I missed Spezi until just now. I could probably make some myself. All I need is orange juice and coke and a little bit of lemonade. Eiric had to stop thinking of the German soda when he heard Reverend Marne repeating his name.

"Eiric, come on up here with your parents. The congregation clapped as Eiric stood and slowly made his way to the front of the church. His parents stood to the left of his pastor, who greeted him with arms spread wide. Eiric accepted a hug from Reverend Marne then stood on his right. Eiric was nervous as he looked out at the congregation as they continued their ovation. He stood at parade-rest, feet shoulder-width apart, and his hands clasped behind his back, looking straight ahead. The people in the audience sat down and became silent at the pastor's direction.

"This is a great day," the minister boomed. His voice carried through the sanctuary without using a microphone. "You all know Eiric was a soldier in the war, fighting for this country! We held prayer meetings every week while he was away, asking the Lord to bring all our military back safely. The Lord used Eiric to help bring a lot of those soldiers back. Now, Eiric hasn't talked about what went on over there and I've refrained from asking him out of respect for him and his parents. Y'all know how modest he's been, all his life."

This was met by more than a few people saying, "Amen."

"I'm sure if you asked him, he would tell you he is no hero. But I'm here to tell you, that I have irrefutable proof that this young man, one of our very own, is indeed, a hero!" Eiric shifted uncomfortably and swallowed hard as he listened to this. Reverend Marne was approached by Deacon Benson, who handed him a green, plastic folder and a smaller dark blue case. Eiric recognized these items immediately as military awards and snapped instinctively to attention.

Reverend Marne opened the green folder and smiled as he read the official letter contained inside. Eiric only heard a few words, "...the Bronze Star Medal... for meritorious service in combat..." The minister continued to read, then added his own words of praise, as the congregation again rose to their feet cheering.

Eiric remained a motionless statue as Reverend Marne opened the blue case, retrieved the Bronze Star, and pinned it over Eiric's heart. Eiric surprised him by rendering a salute. The pastor let out a burst of laughter that he fought to contain as Eiric held the salute in place. Reverend Marne steeled himself and did his best to copy the pose before him. He returned the salute and Eiric dropped his right arm to his side.

They shook hands and then the whole congregation came forward to congratulate him and thank him for his service. They then proceeded downstairs to eat. Eiric found the hunger he had felt earlier during all the hymns and the sermon was now replaced by nausea. He read and re-read the words on the official order, which briefly recounted his actions on the battlefield. He actually had to remind himself to breathe as he stared at the letter.

He unconsciously fingered the medal on his
chest, as if picking at a scabbed-over wound.

Outside the church, Eiric smiled and waved
at his friends and family, as he unlocked the
door to his car. He eased away from the
parking lot and mixed in with the Sunday
afternoon traffic. At the first stop light, he
reached into his glove box and placed his pistol
on top of the green folder on the passenger
seat. Tears rolled down his face as he drove
towards his home.

On the highway, he barely noticed blaring
horns as vehicles swerved to get around him.
He did hear a chorus of screams, gunfire, and
explosions. He didn't see angry truckers waving
their middle fingers at him but he did see
bloody Iraqi soldiers, civilians, and a few of his
friends, falling around him. Pain shot through
his limbs and he felt the car jerk as he drove on
the shoulder of the highway. His car came to a
stop halfway in a ditch.

Eiric's only conscious thought was on the
weight of the pistol, now in his hand. He
screamed and pounded his head with his left
fist, trying to rid himself of the other intrusive

sights and sounds in his head. He knew there was only one way to end it all. He chambered a round and put the muzzle against his suit. The barrel clicked against the Bronze Star over his chest and he looked down at them both. A new stream of tears ran down his face. He squeezed his eyes shut and pounded his temples with both fists, still clutching the loaded weapon.

The tortured faces of the wounded passed before him as if on a conveyor belt. A low-pitched, inhuman sound crawled out of his lungs. When the sound ceased, he raised the gun to his temple. His mother's face chased away the nameless people in his head and he lowered the weapon. The pistol dropped to his lap as a wave of pain coursed through his arms. He clutched his biceps and tried to rock away the pain as he whispered a prayer. "Lord, please forgive me, but I have to end this. I can't take this anymore. I just ask you to be with my family, especially my mom. Help her understand this is the only way."

He reached for his pistol, but instead of picking it up, he accidentally knocked it off the seat. The gun made a dull thump as it hit the carpeted floorboard. Another sound, tapping on the glass to his left and a commanding voice, surprised him.

"Sir, are you alright?" It was a State Trooper. Eiric blinked several times as he looked at the chevrons on the officer's lapels. He then looked slowly at the floor mat, confused by the sight of the pistol. He slowly pushed the gun under his seat with his foot as he nodded in response. "Step out of the vehicle, Sir," the trooper ordered. Eiric opened the door and moved deliberately out of the car.

The officer, noticing Eiric's sweat and tear stained face, flared his nostrils as he sniffed for alcohol. Satisfied that Eiric was not drunk, he continued to inspect him. The trooper's steel-blue eyes, squinting in the shade provided by the over-sized brim of his hat, suddenly widened when he saw the medal on his suspect's chest. *That's a Bronze Star! Holy shit!* "Is this a Bronze Star?" Eiric nodded. *Wow! I knew it!* "You in the military?" Again, Eiric nodded. The officer felt the cool air flowing from inside the mustang and wondered, *why is he sweating so much? He can't be on drugs if he's military. Something's wrong with this picture.*

"My old unit in Germany sent this to my parents. They gave it to our pastor so he could present it to me at church."

"I thought you said you were still in the military? Why did your unit send your medal to your folks?"

"I don't know," Eiric shrugged. "I'm in the Reserves, now, so I don't know why it didn't go to my unit. They just surprised me with it today."

The trooper believed him but still needed to be sure there were no drugs involved. "Can I search your vehicle?" Eiric nodded and the man leaned past him to look inside the car. Eiric thought about the gun under his seat.

Damn! He's looking for my gun. He's gonna have me locked away in a looney bin! This wouldn't have happened if they had just sent this to my Reserve unit!

Eiric's mind went to his new Army Reserve company. Most months, he looked forward to putting on his uniform and going to drill on the weekend. It was the only time he felt like he really belonged, where people respected him and wanted him to be around. Sure, his family was glad he was home safe, but they probably would be happier if he found some other place to have his nightmares. He was excited when EMS hired him, but he was gradually beginning to realize that they only wanted him for his black face. This trooper was no doubt one of their boys out on patrol, waiting to catch him doing something. *What if he thinks I'm trying to commit a crime with my piece? Shit! Why did I have it out?*

"What do we have here?" Eiric froze in the position of attention. He didn't want to give this cop a reason to arrest him. He knew he was going to have to admit he was about to kill himself. The trooper straightened up as he crawled out of the car. "Son, I can't believe my eyes! What the heck were you thinking, putting this in there like that?"

Eiric closed his eyes but couldn't stop the flow of tears coming down. The lawman cleared his throat. He then began to speak. Eric opened his eyes in shock as he realized the trooper was reading from the commendation letter in the green folder. When he finished reading aloud the official paper, the trooper smiled and said, "Sir, I can't believe you just put this down on the seat, where anybody could've plopped down on it! If you don't mind, I want to shake your hand!"

Eiric extended his right hand and accepted the trooper's enthusiastic congratulations. "I have to apologize to you, Mr. Lesson. When I saw your car on the side of the road, I thought you were a drunk. Then, when I saw how you looked, no offense, I thought you were high. I went in your car looking for drugs, but when I saw this," shaking the green folder, "I knew I had made a mistake. Man, you're a hero! Come, on, let me help you get this baby outta that ditch!"

The two men were able to easily push the rear passenger side out of the ditch and onto the shoulder. Eiric thanked the trooper and accepted a business card from him. "I don't know what you're going through, but I know something's wrong. If you ever need somebody to talk to, give me a call!" With that, the trooper returned to his cruiser and left Eiric behind. When the Crown Victoria was out of sight, Eiric retrieved his pistol and put it back in its case in the trunk of the mustang.

The next morning, Eiric was wakened by loud voices in his mother's kitchen. A man's voice, familiar, but out of place, drifted down the hall. *What kind of dream is this? This looks like my room at home, but I swear my mom is talking to somebody who's not here. Okay, this door feels real,* he thought, as he opened the bedroom door. *I can almost taste the bacon out there. This is a trip, I can even feel the cold floor. I must be losing my mind, this seems so real! I can hear birds singing outside, cars going down the highway, and there's his voice again, laughing with my mom.* Eiric shuffled closer to the kitchen. With each step, he feared seeing some grisly image of his mom eating bacon while being shot by an AK-47. He came within eyesight of the dining room and froze. He was ready to scream, but could only let out a hoarse whisper, "Gandhi?"

"On your feet, Soldier!" Gandhi ordered with a smile as he stood from the table. He was wearing his dress green uniform, and though he didn't have half as many medals as Eiric, it was still an impressive sight in his mother's front room.

I'm not dreaming, this is real! That's really Gandhi walking towards me! No way!
"Gandhi? Is it really you? I mean, are you really here? I mean..."

"It's me, E! What's up, Bruh?" Gandhi came up to Eiric and the two men grabbed each other's shoulders and laughed. "Your folks picked me up at the airport this morning! Your mom was gonna wake you up but I asked her to let your lazy as...uh, butt, get some rest! Look at you, a dang civilian, sleeping 'til noon!"

"I can't believe it's really you! I mean, I'm glad to see you, but what are you doing here?" Gandhi's smile faded and Eiric saw the bones in his jaws push firmly against the skin covering them. They released each other as Gandhi looked back at the table. Eiric's mother and father both looked silently down at the table. "What's wrong? They didn't kick you out, did they?"

"No, I'm here on bereavement leave. That's why I tried to call you. Eiric, Man, I got some bad news, Bruh." Eiric felt a cold shiver over his body. He had attempted to call Gandhi after lying to his mother, but some new private he didn't know told him Gandhi wasn't there. At the time, he didn't see the point leaving a message, and just hung up. He looked into his friend's eyes, watering up behind his glasses. "Man, Big Greasy is dead." He paused as Eiric reacted in disbelief. When Eiric asked, he described what had happened.

"Eiric, things got crazy after you left. The Horsemen just wasn't the same with the three of us. Skippy got out a couple of months ago and Big Greasy started showing up late for duty and out of uniform. He couldn't concentrate on his job. I think he was depressed. I couldn't even cheer him up. The only thing that seemed to help him was food. You know, he always loved to eat, but that's all he did. Finally, the captain gave him the boot...gave him a bad conduct discharge for being overweight. When Greasy got home last week, his baby's mama and some dude killed him at his crib! She knew she was his beneficiary, and she knew about the increase in the insurance money since the war. Man, they tried to make it look like a random burglary, but they messed up when they broke the window and the door from the inside of his apartment. I called your mom and told her I needed to tell you something important. I didn't want to tell her all that. I called her again after the funeral and asked if I could come see you."

Eiric sat on the sofa with his head hung low. He had missed his friend's funeral because he was messed up in the head.

"I was the only one of us that showed up. You know Skip's too busy, now."

"Too busy? That was his boy, what do you mean, 'too busy?'" The anger he displayed was directed at himself and seemed a good substitute for the guilt he felt.

"Skip is busy promoting his new book. I guess you didn't know that either. Our boy, Skipper, is a best-selling children's author! Yeah, Mr. Cussing Man was writing books for kids the whole time he was in the Army! I know you heard of *All Kids are Monsters!* That's his series of books! He's got cartoons on TV, video, and I think they're making a movie! He wanted to come, but he couldn't."

The two men sat with Eiric's parents and recalled good times in the past with their friends. It was hard to believe that anyone would want to hurt Big Greasy. Eiric could picture his huge, goofy grin and it made him smile. Of course, he mourned his friend's death but he didn't want to cry, for fear of having a breakdown in front of the others. A single, conspiring tear crept out, leaving a glistening trail down his cheek. He quickly destroyed the evidence with the back of his hand. It was the only tear he would allow to fall for his friend. *Can't see through tears. Can't see through tears.*

Later, after Gandhi had changed into regular clothes, the two men talked about other things. Gandhi started off the conversation, as usual. "So, Bruh, I guess a lot of things changed around here when you left for the service. Let's see, I remember talking with you once about cities in the South having a bunch of Confederate parks and statues. You told me that your town, this town, didn't have any of that, but when your dad brought me here this morning, I saw something peculiar in the city. As we drove by it, I said to myself, 'That's peculiar!' I didn't expect to see anything like that, based on what you told me." He smirked as he looked over his glasses at his friend's disgusted face.

"Fuck you, Gandhi! So, I lied about the statue. You probably already knew that way back then. We didn't ask for that damn thing and I don't know anybody that likes it, except maybe the people I work with. It's been there forever and I've always hated that damn statue! I hate having to drive around him while he sits on that horse, looking down on everybody. Even that horse looks down his nose at you."

"Well, let's do something about it! Look, I've got a couple of weeks of leave left. I really don't want to go home and your parents invited me to stay as long as I like. You know they won't miss me back in Germany. Come on, Horseman! Let's bust a move and turn this mutha out! They brought down the wall around Berlin so we should be able to bring down one little redneck statue!"

"Man, I ain't messing with that statue! You're just visiting, I have to live here. I don't want to get lynched and I damn sure don't want to go to jail for blowing up a deformed piece of rock."

"I'm not talking about blowing anything up. I meant we can petition to have it removed. Remember me, Gandhi, the non-violent one?"

"Oh, ok, so we petition to get rid of Ol' Reb? Let me ask you something. If I go to your room, back in the barracks, and ask you to take down those naked pictures of Vanessa, would you do it?"

Gandhi answered emphatically, "Yes I would! In a heartbeat!" He tilted his head to the side and cracked a smile as he continued, saying, "Of course, I would have to replace her with Vanity, Apollonia, **Vanity**, Janet, ..."

"Right! Come on, Knucklehead, I need to go check on my schedule at work. Plus, I want you to meet a couple of people." Gandhi agreed and they made their way to the station in town. Eiric purposely avoided driving by the monument with Gandhi in the car. He parked by the curb near the entrance to the main office and they went inside the building. A few staff inside the break room called out as they passed by. Eiric introduced his friend before they headed towards the bulletin board. The usual clamor of the breakroom was reduced to background TV sounds as the staff exchanged furtive glances.

The new schedule was pinned to the board beside a flyer for a pot-luck dinner Eiric wanted to attend. When he first heard about it, he asked his mother if she would make a dish for him to take. Of course, she agreed as long as he gave her enough notice in advance. He was assured that the information would be posted on the bulletin board. Now, here it was, the information he had asked for weeks ago. Somebody placed the announcement...days after the meal. He let out a disappointed, "Aww, man," then shifted his attention to the schedule. Eiric's eyes narrowed as he saw only four checkmarks for the next five weeks. "I don't believe this!"

"Man, that's not right! You need to talk to somebody!"

Just then, Robbie walked up to them. "Is there a problem, Eiric? Who's your friend?" *Like I give a shit!* Eiric introduced the two of them then pointed to his name on the schedule. *Dammit! He just had to come in here with his posse right after I posted this!* Robbie drew in a long, audible breath then said, "Let's talk it over in my office." He looked at Gandhi and managed a forced smile as he asked, "Can you wait here? This won't take long." *Hopefully, this will make that nigger quit, and we can get thangs back to normal around here.* Gandhi peered at Robbie over the top of his glasses and nodded.

He watched them closely as they walked to the Training Officer's door. He noticed Robbie's smile transform into a scowl as he opened the door and motioned Eiric inside. He stealthily positioned himself closer as they disappeared behind the closed door. He heard Eiric politely ask about the decrease in his hours. On the way over to the station, Eiric had talked about his job but Gandhi thought some of it was exaggerated. He couldn't believe Eiric would continue to work with these people if half the things he said were true.

You're a better man than me, E. I don't know you tolerate this. You're better than this! Don't these racist bastards realize who you are? You're the man! But they can't see your greatness 'cause it's covered in dark skin. Man, if you were white, they'd put **you** *on that horse in the middle of town!* He shook his head as he listened to the voices inside the room.

"Robbie, this is not fair. I was hired for a full-time position. It's bad enough, I don't get to ride the emergency trucks. But, I can't make it with just four days on the schedule."

"It's not **fair**?" The pitch of Robbie's voice threatened to shatter glass and dogs' eardrums for miles around. "I'll tell you what's not fair." *You uppity nigger!* "It's not **fair** that I have to sort through applications and look-it a person's **'Ethnicity'** before I look-it their qualifications! It's not **fair** that my kids can't go to school and dance to their kinda music at their own prom 'cause all they play is Hippity-Hop! It's not **fair** that honest people with good credit lose out on prime real estate 'cause **some people** come

along with **gub'ment** assistance and steal it out
from under you! 'Fair?' I'll give you 'fair.' You
need to take a closer look-it that schedule! I
ain't playin' no favorites! Somebody else's got
a lot less time than you. And guess what...he's
white! And, he's the one that suggested you
only ride the convalescent truck, so, run tell
that!"

Robbie was right. One other person was
scheduled for fewer days than Eiric. Old Earl,
the tailor shop owner. Before coming to the
office, Eiric's original plan was to ask to be
taken off the schedule, to spend time with
Gandhi and mourn the death of his friend.
With this new schedule, he had all the time he
needed without asking. He apologized for
taking up Robbie's time and turned to leave.
Gandhi moved away from the door before his
friend came out. As they walked to the exit,
one of the paramedics, Jenny, met them in the
hallway. She was excited about some papers
she was carrying.

"Hey, Eiric, who's your friend? He's not
looking for a job, here, is he? You might not get
any hours if he gets hired!" He introduced

them and then she began to share the reason for her happiness. Eiric hoped she would be able to tell her tale without using her favorite term, 'nigger-rig.'

"I'm applying to go to nursing school at Winston-Salem State, you know, y'all's school! Paramedics can get their BS in nursing in a year and a half, just going on Saturdays! And I'll be a **minority** there and get a minority scholarship!" she giggled. Gandhi shot a quick glance at Eiric. "How ya like that? I'm going to let Robbie check out my app, 'cause I don't want anything to go wrong. You know they look at every little, niggly thang!" The men stared at each other through squinted eyes as she walked to the office at the end of the hall. Gandhi shook his head as he tried to imagine what 'niggly' meant.

Two familiar policemen, Lewis and Cardwell, were waiting by the mustang. They looked thrilled to see Eiric's troubled face. "Looky here, it's Super Soldier! I wonder if they'll still throw a parade for you if they know you like breaking the law," Lewis said, pointing to Eiric's car. A narrow slip of paper, anchored by the wiper, flapped against the windshield. The officers smiled politely as they offered advice against operating motor vehicles illegally.

"There's nothing wrong with my car! What's this ticket for?" Eiric demanded.

Officer Cardwell snickered as Lewis answered in a syrupy-sweet tone, "Oh, I forgot. Let me **read** it for you! Hmmm... seems your license plate is missing. Now, you can't be driving around without one of those. Y'all know that!" The cops followed Eiric as he walked to the rear of the vehicle. He looked in disbelief at the empty spot where the plate should be. There was a clear outline of dust that marked the spot.

"Ok, where's my license plate?" Obviously, the tag was removed recently and his voice could not hide his anger.

Lewis feigned shock as he asked, "Are you trying to accuse us of something illegal? You know, people need proof when they throw around accusations about crimes, especially when they point fingers at officers of the law. Without concrete evidence, a person can be held liable for slander. We just happened to be on patrol," w*hen one of your co-workers inside called us,* "when we spotted this car without a license. While we're at it, let us see your licenses," he said, pointing at the two of them. The two men produced the IDs as requested to each of the policemen. The other cop whistled as he inspected Gandhi's NY license.

Cardwell slowly shook his head. He raised his eyebrows, impressed by the words on the card. "Well, well, well! New York City! I don't suppose you have a license to drive in North Carolina?" Gandhi stared at his mouth as he asked this through clenched teeth.

Gandhi replied tersely, "As far as I know, the one you're holding is good all over the US, including North Carolina. It's even accepted overseas, but if you need more, here's my European driver's license, my Government issued P.O.V., Personal Owned Vehicle license, my military ID card, and my military vehicle license. I also have a certificate from a Defensive Driving class I took this year. Will this suffice, Office-Sir?"

Cardwell passed the license to Lewis. Lewis reviewed it then nodded as he returned the cards. "Y'all can go about your business, just get this taken care of."

"What about my license plate?"

Officer Cardwell practically snarled, "You need to keep this ticket handy, in case you get pulled over before you get the plate replaced. It will only cost half as much as an original plate. Then, pay the fine and pay closer attention to your car. Have a good day, Gentlemen."

Eiric and Gandhi got in the car and the ticket was forcefully placed in the glove box. As they drove to Earl's shop, Eiric described his earlier experience with these two policemen. Gandhi shook his head. "Man, you've got to be careful. Your dad gave me some good advice on the way to your crib. He said you wouldn't tell me, so he had to. He said, 'You gotta be careful around here. You need to know how to spot a redneck. Suppose you see a group of white men talking at a gas station. You go up to them and ask for directions. If somebody answers you with their teeth closed, look out!

That's a redneck! If you follow those directions, they might follow you and hang you!' That cop was talking through his teeth."

They parked at the store and found Earl inside, as usual, looking over his inventory. After the introductions were made, Earl looked closely at Eiric and asked what was wrong. Eiric told him about their encounter with the cops.

"So, it's started," Earl stated. "I hope you didn't thank it was gonna end with Robbie re-writin' your report. These boys're mad as a hornet! They're gonna git backatchoo anyway they kin. You-in me have already been whittled away on the work schedule. I'm ok, 'cause I have my shop. I know yer still in the Reserves, but that ain't gone pay all yer bills. I wish I could hire you, but I can't afford another employee. Even if I could, I couldn't pay you much. You need to find another job. Might not be a bad idea for it to be far away from Murfsburg."

"I'm not gonna let anybody run me out of town! I came back home to be with my family, to serve my people, my community! I don't understand why that's such a bad thing, just because I'm not white!" The store fell silent. Eiric fought back tears, thinking, *Man, I can't believe I just said that in front of these two! Gandhi probably wanted to say, 'I told you so!' and who knows what Old Earl had to say.* He looked at the two of them and they each just lowered their heads quietly. "Don't worry about me, Earl. I already put in an application at the dialysis clinic. They asked me if I wanted a job one day when I was picking up Ms. Elizabeth. Besides, I just found out who's been keeping me on the slow truck. It was you."

"I tried to keep you on the Convalescent truck so you could keep yer job. You kept pushin' to ride ALS, puttin' yerself in the spotlight. I told you before, people ain't ready for that 'roun' here. Now, they've cut yer time. Mine too, 'cuz I stuck up for you. Robbie will keep cuttin' til there's next to nuthin' left, as long as he can prove yer still on the payroll. I told you before, everybody smilin' in yer face is not yer friend." Earl warned them both to be careful as they turned to leave.

The bell above the door clanged noisily as the door opened before them. Jazz's face was partly hidden as she used a bundle of uniforms draped over her arms to push it open. Eiric reached out to help her and she heaved the bundle into his arms.

"Thanks, Eiric. Where were you when I needed you outside, lazy bum?" She gave him a peck on the cheek and shook hands with Gandhi.

"Jazz, this is my man, Gandhi." He had told her about the Horsemen and his time in Germany. She looked approvingly at Gandhi and assured him she was a friend. Eiric looked at her clothes and asked, "What's up with all your uniforms?"

"I'm turning them in. I had to quit." Eiric couldn't believe what she was saying. "That damn Robbie tried to hit on me last week and I slapped him. I didn't say anything about it but I found out yesterday that he was filing sexual harassment charges against me! Two others are backing him up, saying I always flirt and try to sleep with them, knowing they're happily married! They said they wouldn't file the papers if I left on my own, so I'm out."

"That's not right!" Eiric was furious. "You can fight this, just tell them the truth! Their stories will fall apart if they find out about the real you."

"So, I should come out just to save my job? Put my personal life out in public and still be treated like a second-class citizen? I'm not as strong as you, Eiric. When I warned you about these racists, you didn't care because you believed in yourself. I can't let this ruin my life! I can still go anywhere and work as an EMT if I leave on my own terms. And I can wait to tell the world all my secrets, but only if I chose to. I love you for being my only real friend on the squad. Be careful, Eiric." Jazz kissed him on the cheek again and took back her clothes. She went to Earl to return the gear and the two Horsemen left his shop and headed to the dialysis clinic.

At the clinic, they went inside the crowded lobby. Gandhi took a seat and Eiric went into the office to talk with the manager. Gandhi waited in the lobby where he could hear patients in the treatment area arguing over what to watch on TV. Eiric returned a short while later with a huge grin and news that he could start work here in two weeks. Before they left, there was one person he wanted to see. He quickly found the person he was looking for. Gandhi cleared his throat as the beautiful woman approached them.

"What's wrong?" Eiric asked as Sheila got closer. Her cherry-red face held watery eyes and flaring nostrils as she fought to control her trembling arms.

"Ms. Elizabeth just pulled me to the side a minute ago. I thought she needed some help but she just wanted to tell me something in private. She was mad because most of the patients want to watch the stories. When I leaned over to her, she whispered, 'How can you stand taking care of them? Niggers are so spoiled, aren't they? We give them everything they want. We let them come in the same stores and restaurants and get the same things we get, and they're still not satisfied. I guess they won't be happy until they completely take over! I don't understand how you, or any self-respecting white person can touch them, even wearing those gloves.' I was so mad I wanted to choke that heffah! She's such a sweet, little lady. I was shocked when she said that. Plus, she actually thinks I'm white!" Sheila's pale skin, blond hair, thin lips, and grey eyes made this a common mistake for white people. Blacks simply, but incorrectly, assumed she was 'mixed.'

Eiric rubbed her shoulder and said, "Forget her. You know who you are." She smiled at him and Gandhi cleared his throat again. "Oh, yeah, Sheila, this is my friend, Gandhi. He's visiting from Germany for a few days..."

"Actually, I'm thinking about moving here. I've only been here a short time, but I've seen so many interesting and beautiful things." He stared deep into her eyes as he held her hand. She blushed and Eiric cleared his throat before telling Sheila he got the job.

"That's great, but what about your other job? You can't quit. We need to have some color on those trucks. Maybe other minorities can get hired there because of you."

"We'll see. We'll check you out later, if that's cool?"

"You know how to reach me. But here's my number, again, in case you lost it." She wrote down her number and handed it to him before the men turned to leave.

"Damn! Damn! Damn! Man, now I see why you didn't want to bring Gabe home! She is fine! That's my boy!"

"Naw, Man, Sheila's just a friend from high school. She only dates darker skinned brothers, like you. That's why I wanted you to meet her. I want you to enjoy your stay here."

"Thank you, my Brother! Country girls are nice! Man, I've been missing out!"

They returned to Eiric's home and changed into running clothes. Eiric enjoyed having someone else to run with. They talked about old times together and of course, Big Greasy and Skip. They sang their favorite cadences as they ran in formation. They talked about beautiful women they knew or wanted to know. Gandhi could not stop talking about how gorgeous Sheila was. Eiric was beginning to feel sorry, sort of, for introducing him to her. After a few miles, they started walking to cool off. "Alright, G, I'll put in a good word or two for you. I don't think she's seeing anybody." *What the hell, if I can't have her, I want my boy to have a chance.*

"I don't care if she is with somebody. I'm Gandhi, dammit!"

As they recovered from their run, their conversation about Sheila was interrupted by a shrill voice crying out, "Niggers!" They stopped and scanned the yards for the source of the inflammatory word, but all they saw was a toddler bouncing a beach ball. As they continued to walk and talk, the word was repeated. They turned around just in time to see the little boy finish yelling, "Niggers!" As soon as they spun around, a man burst from the screen door, jumped off the porch, sprinted past the boy and came to a halt in the middle of the road. He trembled as he aimed a rifle at the two of them. Gandhi began walking away from the man and was voicing his disbelief when he suddenly realized he was walking by himself. He turned around in time to see Eiric take a step towards the armed man.

Eiric lowered his head slightly and stared at the rifleman's firing eye. *I can't believe this.*

We've lived in this neighborhood for six or seven years and this is the first time one of our neighbors has called me that word. And it's a little baby! He's just repeating what he's heard the grownups saying in his house, so I can't be upset with a baby. Wow, I've been running this same route forever, not bothering anybody, smiling and waving as I pass by people while they've been waiting for a chance to pull a gun on me! I'll be damned! I've spent my whole life helping people and trying to be a positive role model. I've been to other countries, where I was mostly treated with respect, because I tried to learn their cultures.

I even went to a freaking war for this country, MY COUNTRY! I put my life on the line, so I could get money for college, so I can go to school to keep helping people. I survived all that bullshit over there just to come home to this? A city where I have to beg for a chance to volunteer my services? Where I can only get a job if the NAACP threatens to sue? And then, even when I get the job that I'm more than qualified for, I have to swallow my pride as they let inexperienced people do more important work saving lives while I provide taxi service!

My best friend calls me a nigger. My coworkers call me that, plus I'm a drug dealing gangbanger to them! I've got cops after me because I caught them screwing up! My family and friends think I'm nuts because I made it through the war unscratched but came back fucked up in the head! Now, I got this asshole redneck holding a gun on me! What are you waiting for? Just pull the trigger and get it over with! The enemy tried to but didn't kill me over there in Iraq. My friend, J-Dog, was going to kill me when he thought I lied to him about Big O. Why not, I've even tried to kill myself. GO AHEAD, SHOOT ME! PLEASE!

Eiric's mind travelled back to the sands of Iraq. As the morning sun pushed away the darkness and filtered through black smoke, evidence of last night's battle began to materialize. Blood, bodies, and body parts littered the sand. Shell casings, soot, and smoldering debris were everywhere. The smell of burnt flesh, oil, and gunpowder clung to the cool morning air like department store cologne on a heavy-handed lounge lizard.

Soldiers, in varying degrees of shock and exhaustion, stood guard around the vehicles parked at the headquarters tent. Over coffee and MRE's, they exchanged stories of fighting that happened in the dark. One soldier, a tanker, described seeing a raghead appear before his tank, aiming an AK-47 at his gunsight. The tanker fired the main gun and all that was left of the man was scorched sand and a puff of smoke.

Another man spoke about the battle at the railroad berm, where a grenade came over the tracks and landed at their feet. Before it detonated, a sergeant scooped it up and slung it back over the tracks at the Iraqis on the other side. The Americans were saved as it exploded over the heads of their attackers. One private trembled as he relived the horror of having his gun jam as he saw a group advancing towards him. He quickly solved the problem and opened fire on the group, only to discover it was a stand of bushes. He let out a nervous laugh, but asked them, "What if?"

As the talk turned to their friend, Big O, who was shot in the first moments of the battle, Eiric hung his head low. They remembered how nice he was. How friendly he was. What a good friend he was. Was, was, **was**! They only spoke of him in the past! Then the unbelievable news, that Big O was dead. Eiric held back tears as he thought, *I let him die. I froze while he was hurt, and I let him die! It's all my fault!* He looked around the makeshift camp until his eyes found J-Dog. J-Dog was focusing bloodshot eyes at Eiric with a look that could only be described as homicidal. *I'm sorry, J! Big O didn't deserve this. I should be the dead one, especially for just standing there looking while my friend lay there bleeding. Cowards like me don't deserve to live!*

As his mind was locked away in the past, his feet continued to carry him towards the man in the street with the rifle.

Gandhi screamed, "Eiric!", but his friend didn't respond. The man with the rifle lifted his head then returned his cheek to the stock of the weapon. A million thoughts flew through Gandhi's mind, but only one had a chance of

saving his friend. As forcefully as he could, he
yelled, "INCOMING!" He watched in relief as
Eiric dove to the ditch on the side of the road.
The man with the gun had a puzzled look on his
face as he lowered the rifle. Eiric had rolled up
into a tight ball, screaming as he hugged
himself. He was already covered in sweat from
their run but now tears streamed down his
face. Gandhi ran to his friend as he began to
convulse. "Help me!" he said to the confused
man with the gun. The man came over and
kneeled beside them as Gandhi tried to protect
Eiric's head.

"What's wrong with him? He ain't gonna
die, is he? Lord, don't let this ni..." he looked
into Gandhi's eyes before finishing. "Don't let
this man die in my yard!" Gandhi rolled his
eyes at the rifle. "Man, it ain't even loaded! I
was just trying to scare you, I didn't know what
y'all were gonna do to my boy! I'll go call 911!"

"No. Not them!" Gandhi barked. "Can you
help me take him home? It's at a place called
the Crossing. I think we should be close, but I
don't really know!"

"Yeah, Man, it's right around the corner. I know exactly where he lives! Let's get him on my truck!" He turned to the house and yelled, "Lisa, bring me that blanket off the sofa, quick!" A thin woman met them at the bed of the truck and threw a dark blanket on the pickup. "I'll be right back! I'm just gonna run them 'round the corner!" The tires kicked up small pebbles that plinked against the side of the truck as they sped off. "Hold on back there!" he cautioned as Gandhi covered and held on to his friend. The convulsions had stopped, but he was still screaming over the sound of the big-block engine.

In moments, their driver was pulling up to Eiric's home. He parked and helped Gandhi take him inside. "You sure he's gonna be alright here? I mean, I can haul ass and take you to the ER!"

Gandhi thanked the man but refused his offer. He was stunned but accepted the man's outstretched hand and shook it before he returned to his truck and sped off. *This place is crazy! He just pointed a gun at us, but then did everything he could to keep Eiric from dying in his yard! He teaches his son to call us niggers, but he tells his woman to bring us a blanket from his house. Then he warns us to be careful as he's driving like a maniac to get us here.*

This Murfsburg is a strange place. They'll shoot you for being on their streets but they'll take care of you if you get sick! They get **offended** *if you're afraid of the unloaded guns aimed at your head! 'What are you cryin' for, the gun was empty! Hell fire, I might give you a heart attack, but at least I'll take you to the hospital afterwards! You niggers are too sensitive!' I wonder, is it always like this?*

Nobody else was home, thankfully. Gandhi didn't want Eiric's folks to see him in this condition. *He* didn't want to see him like this.

"Where am I? Gandhi, is that really you?" Eiric panicked. He was painfully aware that he had trouble deciding what was real anymore. He was relieved when Gandhi assured him he was safe at home after they ran into a 'little misunderstanding' on the road.

Eiric stood up and shook his head, recalling the man with the rifle. "No, Gandhi. That wasn't a 'misunderstanding.' That's reality.

Everything you've witnessed here, the Confederate statue, the racist cops, my coworkers, Sheila's patient, that guy with the gun, and a baby calling us, 'Niggers'...that's my reality. Even my best friend from high school changed into a redneck and called me a nigger!

"The only 'misunderstanding' has been on my part. I've been doing exactly what you said a long time ago. Burying my head in the sand and pretending not to see all this ugliness. I've been fooling myself. And I've looked like a fool. I've pretended that being called a nigger doesn't hurt, you know, 'sticks and stones.' I've stood by with a look of acceptance as somebody else was called nigger, because I was assured that, 'Oh, don't worry, you're not like **them**.' I try to live by the Golden Rule, treating everybody the same way I want to be treated, but they treat me, us, any way they please. I've always been taught, and I *want* to believe, that people will accept you and respect you for your abilities and the way you carry yourself.

"For a while, that's true. People smile and pat you on your back, but as soon as you leave the room...you're just a nigger! If you know how to behave, you're a, 'Good nigger!' If you make good grades, you're an, 'Educated nigger!' If you try to improve yourself, you're an, 'Uppity nigger!' Nigger, nigger, nigger! I'm so tired of that word! Oh, yeah, then **we** make it worse by calling each other nigger! 'What's up, my Niggah? That niggah is crazy! My Niggah this, my Niggah that!'" Eiric let the blanket fall off his shoulders as he stared at Gandhi. "Okay, I give up! Y'all win! I'm a nigger!"

Gandhi's stomach ached at these words. "Yo, stop it! This is not you talking. You just went through some crazy shit, today."

"Yes, it is me!" Eiric snapped. And as sure as my name, there's got to be a change."

"What do you mean?"

"You were right, Gandhi. I've been a sell-out. You can't just sit quietly on the sidelines while your team is getting stomped. I can't keep turning a blind eye, acting like racism is dead. Racism is alive and kicking! It's way past time that I start kicking back!" There was a cold emptiness in Eiric's words that Gandhi didn't recognize. He felt more afraid now than when his friend was walking towards the man with the rifle. "You know the Confederate monument in the middle of town, Ol' Reb?" Gandhi silently nodded as Eiric turned away from him. "I'm going to bring it down or die trying!"

Sticks and Stones

Eiric and Gandhi busied themselves printing flyers and posters over the next two days. They drove around the county in the cover of night, getting their message out. They started a campaign to rid the community of the Confederate monument in the center of town. They drew up a petition and posted it in the local newspaper. The two also scheduled a rally to be held at the base of the statue to gather support for their cause. They knew they had no chance of actually removing the landmark, so they also presented a reasonable alternative. Their actual goal was to have an official memorial dedicated to the slaves that played a huge role in the city and the South's history. If the good folks of Murfsburg defended, and financed, one statue honoring one slice of the past, surely, they would not object to another monument.

Word was spreading of another protest in Murfsburg. People talked about it at barbershops. They discussed it at prayer meetings. They got riled up at gun ranges and golf courses. Heated conversations cooled off quickly in the presence of someone of a different race. Everyone had an opinion.

Some Blacks supported the proposal but opposed the people behind it. "It's a good idea, but he ain't the first one to come with it. We tried the same thing while he was off working for the Man, playing soldier! Now, he's back in town to save us po niggahs! And that other one ain't even from here!"

Other Blacks thought it was a good idea but worried about their safety. "I'm all for gettin' ridda that statue, but what then? These white folks ain't gone stan' 'roun' quietly while their precious statue gets knocked down. And these good ol' boys ain't never gone let us put up a statue for slaves! If it does get built, it won't stay up for long! And how many of us will get beat down, or worse, tryin' to make it happen? I pray for these young bloods, and I'll stan' wittem, but I don't wanna see nobody get hurt!"

Still, a few black people opposed both the message and the messengers. "Why don't they just leave things the way they are? That statue is not bothering anybody. It's just a statue! It's part of this city's history. We've got good jobs, our kids are getting a good education, and we live in nice neighborhoods. We already had the Civil Rights Movement and we won. Nobody is getting lynched, we can ride in the front of the bus, and we can eat anywhere we want! That boy, Eiric, came home a war hero and slipped into a good job, but now he's complaining. That's the kind of thing that hurts black people more than anything. Sorry-ass, ungrateful niggers, that want everything handed to them instead of working for it! No wonder white people hate **them**! Always complaining about something!

"Like I said before, that statue is not bothering anybody. If anything, it's saving lives. You can't just speed down the street, you have to slow down to go around it. Those two rabble-rousers are the ones causing problems. All they're going to do is piss off a few ignorant rednecks. Then somebody will get hurt for no reason. Everything was fine until they started putting up those posters. I'm going to that so-called rally, but I won't be supporting it. I'm going to show White America that there are some good, self-respecting, law-abiding black people that know a little bit about history and care about traditions."

White people in and around Murfsburg had similar feelings. "They do have a point. The Civil War happened a long time ago and it may be past time to just put that kind of stuff in a museum. Or just display that Rebel crap in the privacy of your own home. Hell, I hate having to slow down and drive around that monstrosity, but who's going to pay for moving it or building another statue? Not my tax dollars! If they can find a way to come up with a change that everybody can agree on, and that won't raise my taxes or create more traffic issues, I'm all for it!"

"If you ask me, minorities have taken over this country! Give them an inch, they'll steal a mile! They've got the government in their pockets. They get paid to lay around, doing nothing but make babies and smoke weed! You can't say anything true about them, you can't joke about them, can't arrest them without getting in trouble yourself. It's getting so you can't be white in America anymore! You get called a racist if you shoot a black person for breaking into your home! What kind of bull is that?

"That monument is here to honor our ancestors who fought for what they believed in. This country would still be in the hands of uncivilized Indians if Americans hadn't taken charge to get us where we are now! Are we supposed to build monuments for every minority? Hell, no, let them put up their own monuments in their own countries where they came from! Put up a statue to **honor slaves**? We did them a favor by bringing them here and making them slaves! Ask any nigger you know and they'll tell you they don't want to go back to Africa! Hell, look at Africans...they don't want to be in Africa! That's why they come here! My ancestors fought and earned that statue and I'll fight to keep it!"

Even Jerry had to listen to his father's take on the subject. He had never again mentioned Eiric's name or told his dad about their fight. "Eiric sure has been making a name for himself since he came home! I remember watching y'all play out back, way back when y'all was kids. I knew back then, he was gonna be somebody! I always liked him and was glad he was your friend. Hoped some of him would rub off on you! He's a war hero, been all over the world! Now, he's working 911! You should ask him to help you out. Hell, he might be able to get you on, finally."

Jerry rolled his eyes and opened a beer bottle. He had applied to EMS three times without any response while Eiric was away. "I bet it won't be long, he might be our first Black mayor! I wouldn't put it pass him, he's got potential! Especially the way he's putting together this rally to get rid of that damn relic downtown! You are going to be there with him, right?"

With his back turned to his son, Jerry's dad continued to heap praises on Eiric. Jerry gave up waiting to hear anything good about anything he had ever done in his life. *That's a damn shame! You care more about some nigger, than you do about your own son!* Jerry pressed the opening of the bottle to his lips and left his father talking to himself.

There were isolated pockets of all races that wanted nothing but a chance to promote their own agendas. There were people who just wanted to have their pictures taken or be on TV. Some planned to loot businesses in other areas of town while the police were distracted by the rally. Others planned to come to the march displaying their Southern pride, ready to incite peaceful activists into acts of violence. Trey, the nurse Earl had warned Eiric about, was prepping his followers to disguise their violent intentions with peaceful facades. Still, some people didn't care about any issue, but planned to come simply because they were bored, and this might just be something to do on a Saturday afternoon.

Eiric and Gandhi could hardly contain their excitement as the day drew near. Eiric was focusing all his energies on doing something positive to help his community. He was thankful that he had not had any more "episodes" since the day he and Gandhi were threatened with a gun. He was thrilled, thinking, *maybe this was what I needed all along. This is my chance to wash away my* *cowardice and redeem myself. Big O, I failed you in Iraq, but I won't fail anyone else ever again! My family can finally see me doing something important, here, for them, and everybody else in the county. I'm no longer a bench-warmer. Maybe I can **earn** that award that was given to me. Gandhi was right all along, but I ragged on him for being too militant while he thought I was a sell-out.* He was sure that his friend was proud of the stance he was taking.

Gandhi was stirred up, but in a different way. *What the hell am I doing here? What have I done? I only wanted to see my boy, but I've helped turn him into a fanatic. He's gonna have to live here long after I'm back in Germany. If they let him live! These people are not playing around! They're for real about this shit! E thinks he's on a crusade, and it is cool, in a way, but not everybody believes in his vision.*

*I talk a good game, but it's just talk. He **believes** in this and is putting his life, our lives, on the line. Can't he see the way people are looking at us? Doesn't he hear what they're saying? I've got to try and convince him that* *it's not too late to reconsider this rally, but I don't know how. Skippy is too busy being a star. Greasy is dead. I can't lose Eiric, too! Hell, it's not just rednecks he has to worry about. His own people are giving him the evil-eye!*

These worries filled his head but his face never betrayed him when his friend talked about the future in Murfsburg after their protest. Eiric was convinced that all parties would realize the changes he proposed would result in a win-win situation, giving everybody something to be proud of. Since he was convinced the divisive structure would never be removed, a new work of art would be created to coexist and take its place to honor Black heritage. Blacks should use the same rationale of trying to honor their dead and keep history alive that white people use to continue to fly their rebel flags and build hateful edifices. Gandhi didn't think Eiric was crazy, even when he was having flashbacks, but his perception of reality was skewed.

Thursday night, two days away from the rally, Eiric and Gandhi were joined for dinner by

two beautiful women, Sheila and Renee. Eiric
had arranged the double date, intending to get
to know Renee better as Gandhi and Sheila did
the same. On the way to the restaurant, he
reminded Gandhi about the first time he met
Renee. "She is a stripper, but I think she's nice,
so don't judge her."

"I'm cool with that. It's just a job. Plus, if
you say she's cool, she's alright with me."

Sheila was already waiting for them inside
the restaurant when the two men arrived. She
was breath-taking, with her blond hair
cascading to her shoulders, perfectly framing
her face, accented with just a touch of make-
up. She was tastefully dressed in a form-fitted
blouse, and pencil skirt. They sat beside her,
leaving the fourth chair open for Renee. Sheila
glanced around the room, observing people
watching the three of them.

Two men at the bar jerked their heads away
and looked towards a basketball game on TV as
she turned her gaze on them. She tried to
shake these two men from her mind but the
angry looks on their faces kept nagging at her.
She smiled politely and turned back to Eiric and

Gandhi as they made small talk, captivated by her, until Renee walked into the building.

Her jet-black hair was bone straight and could easily be seen making a pendulous motion as it ran down to the small of her back. Her brown skin was the perfect matte for the selection of paints applied. She caught the attention of everyone in the room, especially with her bright orange, strapless dress. Every eye watched as she approached the table where Eiric was standing, waving to her.

He was a bit offended when he noticed Renee's reaction upon meeting his friend. The dilation of her pupils and widening of her smile at the site of Gandhi could not be ignored. The confident grin Gandhi had on his face while he chatted with Sheila disappeared when Renee approached the table. His glasses seemed to fog and Eiric could have sworn he heard his usually eloquent friend stutter when he addressed Renee for the first time. Gandhi quickly regained his composure as Renee sat down and assumed being equally as charming to each of the ladies.

They ate and enjoyed each other's company, with Gandhi directing most of the conversation. "So, if you could have anything you wanted in a movie about black people, what would you want to see?"

"I'd like to see a strong, handsome, smart, chocolate Brother. A hero, but he can't be in the military," Renee answered, as she looked keenly at Gandhi. "We can have strong men that don't necessarily have to be soldiers." He sipped from his glass and nodded at her before Eiric spoke.

"Black love. Real love, where the man and woman are just drawn to each other and nothing can come between them. You know, where the man chases down his lady, and doesn't stop until he gets her. And I'm not just talking about sexing her, I'm talking about making her his own."

Gandhi frowned as he put his glass down. "Man, I was gonna say the same thing! No, seriously, I want to see a movie where black people help or save **themselves**. I'm sick and tired of seeing minorities in trouble until some cool white dude shows up to save the day.

Hollywood seems to think we need a 'White' in shining armor because we can't help ourselves. You know what I mean? What about you, Miss Sheila?"

Sheila was nervously twisting her napkin beneath the table when all eyes turned to her. The two spies at the bar clumsily looked away when she turned to them. Sheila tried to ignore them as she smiled at her dinner party. She drew in a deep breath and brought her right elbow to rest on the table top. She placed her jaw slowly in the palm of her hand and said, "Oh, I don't know. I guess I'm just tired of seeing the black person die."

Gandhi clapped his hands and raised his glass. "I'll drink to that!" They each picked up their drinks and joined his toast. He slurped loudly, smacked his lips, and let out a lingering, "Ahhh," sound. The women giggled and Eiric rolled his eyes to the ceiling. Gandhi was the perfect dinner guest, making the ladies feel at ease, like they all had known each other forever. It was not difficult for Eiric to quickly get over his moment of jealousy.

I wish I could be that smooth. Look at them, they love this fool! That's my boy! Shoot, I can't be mad at him. I could have gone out with Renee long before he came to visit, but I couldn't get up the nerve to call her until he came. Actually, Eiric felt he was able to do anything when Gandhi was around. *I'm glad he's here. It's just like old times!*

At this thought, Eiric swallowed hard. A picture of the Four Horsemen, popped into his head. He saw himself seated in a bar in Germany with Gandhi, Greasy, and Skip. Gandhi was preaching about something nobody was listening to. Big Greasy was devouring peanuts and tossing some at unsuspecting people in the bar.

Skippy was cursing, as usual, after returning from the men's room. The whole table laughed at him when he revealed that he had splashed water on his pants while washing his hands, but a woman he met on his way back to the table thought it was pee. Eiric smiled to himself at the thought then excused himself to go to the restroom. Sheila's eyes followed him as he walked away. She warily directed her gaze on the two men who had been paying too much attention to their table, as they left their barstools and trailed Eiric.

Eiric was positioned in front of a urinal when the two large men entered. One paced in front of the stalls, checking for occupants while the other man stood behind Eiric. Eiric would not have paid attention to either of them, but the urinals on either side of him were empty when they both posted themselves at his back.

The man closest to him began to speak. "What's up, Lil Man, you dat Brotha that was in da Army, right?" Eiric nodded and the man continued. "Yeah, you da one workin' for 911! You in yo boy havin' dat protest march this Saturday!" He turned to his partner, who stepped up a little closer behind Eiric. "See, I told you it was him." Eiric tried to finish faster, but he couldn't. He felt extremely vulnerable in this position.

"You right, Dog!" replied the other man as he hunched his burly shoulders. Eiric felt hot breath and spit on his neck as he spoke. "Hell, I don't know if I should ask for his autograph or just beg to shake his...hand. Ha, ha, ha, ha!"

Eiric did not like this man's joke or his sinister laugh.

The man continued. "You know, you in yo boy out there might thank y'all da shit, rollin' in a fat ride, eatin' wit those fine-ass ho's! Even got yo-self a white gal out there, but you tryin' to be Martin Lutha Kang! Y'all makin' all da money in da Army and everythang, but y'all fuckin' thangs up fo everybody else 'round here! I saw you ridin' 'round on those ambalamps, grinnin' in yo lil fancy uniform, speedin' in gettin' **paid in full** while da rest of us niggahs can't keep a job! I got laid off dis week, Motha Fuckah, 'cause a dat lil shit you got planned dis weekend!"

Eiric had just finished the last few drops when the first punch hit him in the right flank. Even though he had tried to steel himself for a fight, he winced and almost blacked out from the pain. The two men worked as a team, punching and kicking Eiric, as he fell to the sticky, urine coated floor. He tried to cover his vulnerable spots but the two larger men were experts at finding new targets. The two finally stopped beating Eiric, pausing only to empty their bladders on him before they left. He was bleeding from his nose and mouth but he was thankful for the taste of his own blood. It washed away the taste of their urine.

Sheila stood up as soon as she saw the two men hastily retreat from the men's room. *Something's wrong! I knew it!* She now regretted not saying anything before to Gandhi as the two men rushed towards the front door. Gandhi's back was to the restroom and the two men leaving the restaurant. He wouldn't have noticed the men even if they had jumped up and danced naked on their table. He was totally absorbed in looking at the two women, especially Renee. "Gandhi! Eiric's in trouble!"

Instantly, the spell was broken. Gandhi snapped to attention and ran to the restroom. He burst inside and saw his friend using the lip of the urinal to try to pull himself off the ground. "What the hell!" he yelled as he ran over to Eiric. As he got him to his feet, he demanded, "Who the fuck did this? Where are they? I'll kill those fucking rednecks!"

Sheila and Renee were standing in the open doorway, sickened by the sight of Eiric's bloody face. Sheila ran inside and helped Gandhi get Eiric to a sink. She began to wipe his face with wet paper towels as a crowd gathered at the doorway with Renee.

"They weren't rednecks, Gandhi!" she cried. "They were two big, black guys that just ran outside! They've been watching us all night!" Gandhi threw his glasses on the counter and pushed his way through the crowd at the door. He ran through the dining room and burst through the main door looking for the two men. He screamed helplessly into the night as he realized he was too late to find them.

He went back inside, where his bloody friend was being helped to their table by the ladies and a waiter. As he made his way to them, he overheard several patrons as they commented on the scene. "We can't even enjoy a nice, peaceful dinner at a nice restaurant without these animals ruining it! They just don't know how to act!"

"You said it! Why can't they go eat and tear stuff up at their own restaurants?"

"Serves him right, coming in here with that White trash! Look at her, fawnin' all over that nigger! He wants to be a Civil Rights activist, causing trouble and tearing down our statue, but he can't even date in his own race!"

"Harold, I told you those black guys were up to no good, the way they ran out of here! I knew something was wrong, the way they kept looking at that table. Look at that poor guy! They beat the crap out of him! And he's black, too! I just don't understand it! I can't eat, let's just go home!"

"Ok, Baby! Let's at least pay for their bill before we go! It just don't seem right. I wouldn't want to have to pay after getting beat up like that."

Gandhi looked at this man, not knowing what to say. He fought back angry tears as he thought, again, *what kind of place is this? I'm so confused! Those Brothers, who probably know Eiric, beat the shit out of him but this white guy who doesn't know Eiric, wants to help out. I've got to stop Eiric before he gets himself killed!*

He went to the table where Sheila was applying ice to Eiric's face. Renee handed him his glasses and wanted to know if he found the guys who did this. "No, they got away! I'm sorry, Eiric! I let you down, Man! I should have gone in there with you! I shouldn't have pushed you into all this mess!"

Eiric let out a pained laugh. "Man, what were you gonna do, hold my hand in the john? I don't need a bodyguard. We both would've got our asses kicked!"

"This is my fault! Eiric, if I wasn't always messing with your head about you being color-blind and talking all that Black Power BS, you wouldn't be sitting here like this! I sit back and talk junk about outdated ideas, racist practices, and hurtful words and I try to come up with clever phrases to make myself sound smarter than some ignorant bigot! But this shit is real! In New York, I only have to worry about gang bangers and cops that think I'm a banger. Here, you've got to look out for rednecks, cops, paramedics, cooks, neighbors, friends, hell, everybody! We've got to cancel Saturday! What good is it if you get yourself hurt worse than this? Or killed, over what, a damn statue? Hell no! We lost Big Greasy over some bull. I wasn't there to protect you, but you survived front-line combat without a scratch. I'll be damned if I let you get killed right here at your crib! We're calling this thing off!"

Eiric slammed his fist on the table. "No! We ain't calling off nothing! I'm not letting anybody, or anything, stop me, Man!" He was already yelling, but he made sure everyone in the building heard him as he continued. "I'm not dead and I don't plan on dying, but if I do, it's worth it!" Sheila let out a pained moan and ran out of the restaurant. Eiric looked at Renee and Gandhi and calmly said, "Y'all can leave, too, but I'm not quitting."

Gandhi looked down at his feet, wondering, *what have I done? Is it me or is it this place? It doesn't matter. I can't let him do this alone.* He clenched his jaws tight and lifted his head to look in his friend's eyes. "I'm with you, Eiric. Horsemen...Forever!" They shook hands and Renee helped him get Eiric to his feet. They tried to pay their bill, but the waiter informed them it had already been taken care of. They made their way out of the restaurant and Renee helped Gandhi get Eiric to the passenger side of his car. They covered the seat with towels he kept in the trunk for cleaning the car.

After they helped him inside, Gandhi walked Renee to her car and they talked for a short while. Eiric smiled and shook his head side to side as he watched her kiss him on the cheek. Gandhi pulled her close and gave her a real kiss, then slowly walked back to the mustang. Gandhi slid behind the wheel with a satisfied smirk on his face. Eiric could have sworn he heard his friend humming. Eiric managed a laugh, and said, "See, it wasn't a total loss. We got a free meal and you got both the girls!"

"You know, you're either the smartest idiot or the dumbest genius in the world! That girl is in love with you. I knew it when I first saw the way she looked at you."

The word, "Okay," crawled out of his mouth. "She loves me, but she kisses you?"

"Just like I thought...you're the dumbest genius! I'm not talking about Renee, idiot! I'm talking about your girl, Sheila. The way she ran out...she loves you, Bruh! I saw that at the clinic that first day you introduced us. I kept telling you how beautiful she was because I was testing you. I couldn't believe you couldn't tell she wanted you. I mean, Man, the way she checks you out is obvious to everybody but you, you knucklehead! You were being nice, trying to set me up with her, but I was trying to make you see what you were passing up! That girl doesn't want me or anybody but you. But, if you really want to be with Renee," he said, before swallowing hard, "I'll back off. I'll be going back to Germany, anyway, so she'll be all yours."

Eiric's head was full of thoughts of Sheila, and how they had always been just friends. All of a sudden, thanks to Gandhi, she was all he could think about. "Naw, Man, Renee likes me, but she **likes** you. I only met her once before, so I don't even know her, really."

"Whew, thank God!" Gandhi yelled. "Man, I'm telling you, that woman is gonna be my wife! I can't go back home, so I might as well move here! I'm telling you, she's the most beautiful woman on Erf! You heard me, E-R-F, Erf!" They laughed as Gandhi began driving for home. "Look here, E, if you're still serious about us doing this thing Saturday..."

"I'm serious, Gandhi! Nothing is gonna make me change my mind now! I just got my ass kicked in a bathroom! If we stop now, it means I got piss all over me for nothing!"

"Ok, Eiric. We just gotta be more careful. Anywhere we go, we go in pairs. Agreed?" Eiric, too tired to argue and too sore to keep speaking, nodded his head. "There's just one more thing." He looked over the top rim of his glasses at his friend. "We gotta roll down the windows, 'cause, Man...you stink!" They both laughed as the windows went down.

Eiric's family was watching TV when Gandhi entered the house, supporting his wounded friend. They sprang from their seats and rushed towards them to help. They stopped short, holding their noses, gagging, coughing, and fanning the air.

"What the...?" was all Eiric's dad could force out. Gandhi told them about the fight at the restaurant as Eric's mother cleaned and inspected his bloody face. Eiric's siblings watched him with wide, unblinking eyes as the adults continued to speak. "Ok, that's it!" Eiric's father yelled. His eyes fixed on Gandhi. "Everything was fine until you showed up. I don't know how you did it, but I know this is your fault! This whole rally business was your idea. Look at him; you happy now? You can do what you want, but my boy is not going downtown Saturday!"

"Yes Sir. You're absolutely right. It's all my fault. I'm sorry this happened to him. I wish it was me instead. We'll call it off."

"At Ease!" Everyone was stunned into silence by Eiric's loud command. "Look, I know y'all care about me and everything, but I'm a grown man. I make my own decisions. In case y'all forgot, I'm a soldier, and I've been through combat, so I think I know how to take care of myself!"

He tracked his father's raised eyebrows and continued. "This is nothing. Those two dudes literally caught me with my pants down. You and Mama taught me everything about being a good person, a responsible adult. The Army taught me how to be a real man. Gandhi showed me how to use my voice. This is important to me, more important than that war in Iraq, fighting for somebody else. Everybody keeps thanking me for going over there, but I don't know why! Are they thanking me for killing people? Really, that's all we did! I don't even know what to say, except, 'You're welcome.'"

Eiric looked around at everyone before continuing. "I'm going to do this with or without you. It might not accomplish anything. But what if it does?"

Eiric's mother looked at her son and then at her husband. "We'll be there. All of us! I'm tired of looking at Ol' Reb, anyway," she laughed. Gandhi and Eric's father looked at each other bemused. After shaking hands with them, Eiric headed down the hall towards his room and the shower.

Eric's father put his arm on his wife's shoulders as he spoke in a calmer tone to Gandhi. "You'll be with him?"

"Yes Sir! I got his back, all the way."

They shook hands and said their good-nights before Gandhi followed his buddy's path down the hall. Eiric's parents hugged each other then went back to their seats to be with their other children. They looked at the TV screen, where a comedy was showing, but in their heads, other images played. Scenes from the Civil Rights marches in the 60s played out. Some of the images were peaceful marches, with singing and praying, while others were full of water hoses, biting dogs, and Blacks beaten with batons and sticks.

They saw smoke trails from SCUD missiles shot down over Saudi Arabia and sand-colored tanks, with upside-down Vs, carving long scars in the desert sand. Yellow ribbons adorned everything as civilians waving flags saluted soldiers marching in formation. Klansmen, in spotless white uniforms, held flaming torches high above their pointed hoods. Cars, trucks, bicyclists, and pedestrians slightly altered their routes, to circle a Confederate monument in the center of the busiest intersection in town. A black man in tattered clothes, eyes bulged and covered in flies, dangled beneath a gnarled, hate-filled tree limb, suspended by a taught noose. In the Lesson home, the Nielson rating plummeted, as the family abandoned the TV for bed.

Eiric and Gandhi sat on their beds finalizing plans for the rally. They had no idea how many people would attend, if any. They were sure the police would be present, so they weren't too concerned about safety. They were more focused on making sure they had their permit and that they would not be turned away. They had put the word out to have everyone off the street, but not block pedestrian traffic or entry to stores along the sidewalk. Above all else, this was to be a peaceful event. If any violence erupted, the rally would end, and Eiric would be forced to give up on his quest to bring down Ol' Reb.

Gandhi was nodding his head, looking towards the window. Through the curtains, he saw yellow flares bobbing in the dark outside. His spine stiffened as he felt the air in the room suddenly sucked out. He had read many stories about ghost figures, clad in white shrouds with pointy hoods. They carried ropes and guns to terrorize Blacks and other minorities. They marched with torches to illuminate the night sky before making a cross come to life in a fiery blaze. He pointed his finger and hoarsely gasped, "The Klan! It's the Klan, the real life KKK!"

Eiric instinctively snatched a flat, black box from underneath his bed. He turned the key, already in the lock, and opened the case. He wrapped his right hand firmly against the grip of his pistol and slammed a full magazine into the weapon. He chambered a round and, crouching, followed the barrel over to his window. Gandhi was right beside him, wishing he had the other gun that was out in the glove box. He eased himself up to peek outside. The pistol was ready to take out as many as sixteen invaders. His eyes darted side-to-side before he whispered, "I don't see anybody!"

"Man, I saw a bunch of torches out there! Maybe they went to the front yard!"

"Torches? Look out there, is that what you saw?" Gandhi stood up, then quickly squatted, nodding his head. Elric lowered his pistol and laughed out loud. He walked back over to his bed and safely unloaded the weapon, still laughing. He placed the pistol back into its cradle and secured the box beneath his bed. Even in the dark, he could see that Gandhi was getting angry. He finally said, "Go back to bed. Those are not torches, and there are no Klansmen out there. Those yellow lights are lightning bugs! I mean, fire flies! Good night, City Boy!" Eiric laughed as he snuggled beneath his sheets.

Gandhi stood there a moment trying to process the words he just heard. He had no idea what Eiric was talking about but he followed his advice and went over to his own bed. *A firefly? I thought that was somebody who starts fires.* He suddenly remembered that there really was a flying insect that lit up the night, searching for a mate, with its fluorescent butt. He rolled his eyes and smacked his forehead, as he also remembered that an arsonist was sometimes called, a firebug.

All, Fall Down

Sometime later, in the deepest, darkest part of night, Gandhi was jolted out of a peaceful slumber by a loud scream. He lay motionless, clutching his pillow. He held his breath as his eyes darted around scanning the room in the darkness. He looked over at Eiric's bed. *Where are my glasses? Is he messing with me about those fire flies? Is somebody breaking in? Is it really the Klan this time? Why is he just lying there, didn't he hear...?*

His thought was interrupted by another shriek. Even without his glasses, he immediately honed in on the source. Eiric was crying out in his sleep, just like in the barracks. Looking back to those nights on post when he stood outside Eiric's door, he was suddenly thankful that he never experienced it this close up before. Unsure of what to do, and more afraid than he cared to admit, he placed his glasses on and slipped out of the bed. Moving silently, he made his way out of the room, gently closing the door behind him. He turned to the kitchen and was both surprised and relieved to see Eiric's parents sitting at the table. He joined them and Eiric's father poured him a cup of coffee. "Thanks. So, what's up?" he asked nervously.

Eiric's mother spoke as his father motioned with his head towards Eiric's room. "Was he like that in Germany? I mean, crying like that? What happened to him?"

"Ma'am, I don't know what happened to him! He wasn't like this before the war. I mean, he was the most patriotic, most gung-ho soldier in our unit. He's the nicest guy in the world, but he was made to be a soldier. He's a medic but he learned how to do everybody else's jobs, artillery, infantry, commo, you name it. When we went to the field, it was like he was home. He never slept in a tent, just outside on the ground, under a vehicle, or in a tree! One night, during war games, he saved us from an attack because he was outside and heard the Op-For team sneaking into our camp. He took out six of them without firing a shot."

They looked at him with raised eyebrows. "We had blanks, not real bullets. It was like laser tag. We had special laser devices on our weapons and everybody wore sensors that made a loud noise and lit up red when you got hit. Anyway, he tied up two of them and got the other four by saying, 'Close Kill,' which basically means you're stabbed to death. That was before he started shooting! The people on guard duty opened fire and that woke everybody else up. We won the battle that night but Eiric got in trouble with the refs because he tied up those two dudes. You're not supposed to fight or put hands on each other. They said he broke the rules, so they sent him to a POW camp...but he escaped the next day and came back to camp!"

Gandhi laughed at the image of Eiric digging under a fence and running four miles back to their campsite. "So, escaping the enemy was also against the rules, so the refs tried to get him busted for that, but our commander said he did what every soldier is trained to do. If you get captured, you try to escape!"

"That's my boy!" said Eiric's dad.

"Oh, that's nothing. Before the war, he was working on going Special Forces. He wanted to be an 18 Delta, Special Forces Medic. He was afraid of heights, so he would go out, by himself, to our confidence course after work. That fool was climbing the high tower, a little bit higher each time, until he made it to the top. He was getting his mind right for jump school. He had it all planned out. He was mad that he couldn't volunteer to go to Panama, when we went after Noriega. He was in a PLDC, a leadership class, when the call for medics came over. Nobody else volunteered, but he wanted to. He was livid, thinking his skills were being wasted, but he couldn't give up his spot in school.

"I was in PLDC when Desert Shield started and they needed medics to go over. He was the first to volunteer. He even demanded to be with the Scouts, so he would be sure to see some action. He didn't come to tell me, I guess because he knew I would try to talk him out of it. He was right, I would have. War games are one thing, but actually going to war is another level. We went to the field a lot, to be ready in case war spread to Germany, but we wrote to him almost every day. He was actually enjoying himself during Desert Shield, going on combat patrols, sneaking into Iraq, blowing up stuff before the ground war started. Then the letters stopped and we didn't hear from him until he was coming back to the G. Germany. Watching the news didn't help, because they never mentioned the unit he was assigned to until it was all over."

"Yeah, we went through the same thing," Eiric's mother recalled. "They talked about them before they went over and then nothing until after the war ended. After they did the Hook into Iraq and forced the Cease Fire. He called us a couple of days before he flew back to Germany to tell us he was ok. I'll never forget that feeling."

"Relief," Eiric's dad stated. "We didn't get letters or news, either."

"Something changed him over there. I tried to ask him about it, but I always change the subject because he always gets this look on his face. It's like he's sitting there with you, but his mind is somewhere else. He doesn't smile as much. I mean he smiles but it's kind of, fake, like he's forcing it. He gave up trying to be a Green Beret. Whenever anybody mentioned it, he would just get quiet or go off by himself. He didn't get hurt in Iraq, but he always seems so, I don't know...full of pain. You know what I mean?" They nodded silently. "He still tries to have a good time, but it's like he can't be relaxed and enjoy sh...I mean, stuff, like he used to." Gandhi looked embarrassed. "I talked him into going to Mental Health on post, but then that turned out bad. I was glad when he decided to get out but I was worried when he said he was going to stay in the Reserves. I thought he would be better when he came home and got to be with you and his old friends, but I see he still needs help. I don't know what else to do."

They agreed that Eiric needed their prayers, their support, and to just, "Be there for him." Eventually, the cries went away, and they went back to bed. For a long time, Gandhi lay silently watching his snoring friend, punishing himself for ever going to PLDC. He eventually dozed off but a good night's sleep eluded him, as he woke up to check on his friend whenever the bed squeaked or Eiric's pattern of snoring changed.

Eiric was already dressed when Gandhi rolled out of bed the next morning. "Afternoon, soldier! Thought you were gonna sleep the day away."

You're joking, right? Just like before, he doesn't remember a thing. How can anybody scream like that and not know it? "How you doing? You look like you're moving around pretty good."

"I'm sore but I'll live." The look on Gandhi's face made him wish he had said something different. He remembered their talk on the drive home last night and changed the subject. "What time did you say you were supposed to meet Renee? I want to go see Sheila."

"She said twelve, at that ice cream café." He was getting his gear to head to the shower.

"Okay, cool. I know you want us to roll together, but I need to talk to her privately. I'm sure you don't want me hanging around while you get your mack on. I can drop you off there, go see Sheila on her lunch break, and come back to get you later." Gandhi considered this as he bit his lower lip. "Come on, Bruh, it's broad daylight. Just sit with your back to the wall and scan your perimeter."

All of a sudden, he saw sand dunes bathed in subdued sunlight. It was late afternoon, and a sand storm had just ended, allowing a better view from his window of the hummer. The barrel of his M-16 rested on the lower ledge of the open window as he scanned the perimeter to their left. Every few feet, he saw white PVC pipes, air tubes, protruding from the sand as they drove slowly forward. A small voice fought to be heard over the static of the radio, urging the Scout Platoon to move faster ahead of the tanks. Eiric shook his head forcefully to rid his mind of these images. Gandhi was mumbling something, unaware of the show in Eiric's head. Dazed, Eiric asked, "What did you say?"

Damn! He was off in Iraq, again. I should've known! He had that look on his face. "I said it sounds like a plan. Let me bust a move so we can roll out."

Gandhi left the room and Eiric slumped to the floor. *Lord, help me! I don't want to keep going back there!* He thought about the vision he had moments ago and closed his eyes tight.

He struggled for breath as he recalled the stinging sand forcing its way through the bandana that covered his nose and mouth. He rocked himself as he remembered how helpless he had felt as they inched head first into the sandy blizzard. There was no way to tell if they were headed for the enemy, surrounded by them, or driving right by them. Their only guide was a small, electronic device, something called a GPS. It told them they were on track to meet the Iraqis. He remembered tapping his trigger finger on the trigger of his rifle, with the safety engaged, as he squinted at his assigned perimeter through useless goggles. He recalled wanting to be ready to flip the safety off in case an unfriendly image appeared. He opened his eyes and looked down at his right fist. His index finger was tapping against his thumb.

It didn't take Gandhi long to get dressed, so Eiric was still on the floor when he returned to the room. He used the bedframe to push himself up and straightened his clothes. They then baptized themselves in cologne before leaving the room. As they made their exit, they could hear Eiric's mom coughing as she yelled, "Y'all trying to kill me!"

Eric's little red time machine took them to the ice cream shop in no time. Eiric pumped up the stereo as he pulled away, leaving Gandhi alone with Renee. *He's right about one thing, she is fine!* He quickly turned his mind to thoughts of what he wanted to say to Sheila. She didn't know he was coming, but she had a flexible lunch and he was sure he could see her. He was talking out loud, practicing a speech to her when he saw another driver look at him strangely. *Oh, no, now I'm talking to myself. I am going crazy! What the...I'm being paranoid, too! Ain't nobody paying attention to me! That fool probably didn't even see me!*

He didn't notice a silver Grand Prix following him. It parked across the street as he parked at the clinic. He didn't see them, but five pairs of eyes were fixed on him as he went inside.

The clinic's secretary was seated at her desk facing the lobby entrance when he walked in. She opened the sliding glass and called out to him. He went over and asked for Sheila. "Ok,

Hon, hold on a second while I call her. She's in the breakroom. You want to go back there, or do you want her to come up here?"

"Out here, if she's able to come." The secretary batted heavily made-up eyelashes and smiled as she called Sheila to the lobby over the PA system. Eiric thanked her and stepped away from the glass shield. A few minutes later, Sheila stepped into the lobby wearing a curious look on her face. The expression turned serious when she spotted her visitor. His smile faltered slightly as he observed the change on her face, but his voice was steady.

"Hey! I hate to bother you while you're working, but I really need to talk to you. If you can't, I'll understand."

She folded her arms over her chest and stated, "You can talk. I've got a while before I have to go back on the floor." He looked over her shoulder at the secretary's office, where a small crowd of co-workers had gathered to watch them. He reached out for her elbow and gently led her outside the building. They stood in the shade as he began his speech.

"Look, I don't like to beat around the bush, and I know I'm not as smooth as Gandhi, but I want you to know something. I really like you. No, that's not it. Sheila, I love you! Last night made me realize I always have. I've dated lots of other girls, but deep down, I guess I always wanted you to be mine."

"Ok, so why didn't you ever ask me out? Hmm? The only reason you asked me yesterday was so you could pass me off to your buddy. Now, all of a sudden, you love me?"

"No, it wasn't like that! I mean, I did ask you out for Gandhi, because I thought you really liked him when y'all met. He seems like your type..."

"What do you mean, my 'type?'"

"You know, he's darker brown, smooth talk..."

"You think he's my type because he's darker than you?"

"Well, I've only seen you with dark-skinned Brothers, so I thought that's what you liked."

"Eiric, you're talking about high school! I dated those guys because those two were the **only** boys that asked me to go with them. They were nice, but I would've dated anybody that was nice to me. Somebody started that stupid rumor that I only wanted dark-skinned boys because I was so light! Eiric, was that you that made that up?" He frowned and shook his head. "But you believed it?" He shrugged his shoulders then nodded slowly as his shoulders slumped down. "That's why you never tried to get with me? I always thought, one day, you would finally stop trying to be my friend and tell me how much you wanted me. I thought something was wrong with me! You made me feel like something was wrong with me!" Tears started to form, but she refused to let them fall. "You didn't even write to me while you were gone, not even during the war!"

He reached out and snatched her close to him. Water slid down her cheeks and he tasted salty tears as he leaned in and kissed her mouth. He was relieved to find she was kissing him back. Moments later, he pulled away and smiled at her. "So, I told you that I love you and you didn't say anything." *'I love you, too, Eiric!' would be nice!*

"You're right. I really, really **like** you and I...don't look like that!" she scolded as his smile flattened. "I want to love you, but I want to make sure I know you. I can't just go crazy over you because you came home and finally looked at me. Those other women might fall for it, but I need more than a kiss! Even though, it was a good kiss." *It was better than I ever imagined it would be! You might have been a nerd in school, but you're a damn good kisser!* "I want to get to know you again, Eiric. I don't want to see you get hurt again. Last night was too much, now you're about to put yourself in danger tomorrow!"

He stopped her. "Nothing is gonna happen to me! I'm a little sore, but they didn't hurt me that bad. They got lucky, that's all! I love you, even if you don't love me...yet!"

She closed her eyes, puckering her lips, as he leaned in for another kiss. Her eyes popped open as she barely felt his soft lips touch her forehead. He maintained contact with her skin as he lowered his mouth and kissed her left eyelid. *Oh my God! Nobody has ever kissed me like this!* Her legs were beginning to wobble when he released her and turned away. She watched him as he walked steadily toward his car. She glanced at the clinic door when one of her co-workers tapped the glass, grinning and waving at her. She stuck out her tongue then turned her attention back to Eiric as he got closer to his car. *Oh no!*

Across the street, she saw five men, two of them from last night, climb out of a silver car. She had to go back inside to her patients but she couldn't move. Panicking, she screamed, "Eiric!" He spun at the sound of her voice and winked at her. Her face was pained and she frantically pointed towards the men across the street. Eiric snapped his head to see what she wanted him to see. *Ok! Good, now hurry up and get in your car and go straight home!* They were punching their palms, flipping middle-finger salutes, and waving Eiric to come over. One of the men from the restaurant pointed an imaginary gun at Eiric and jerked his index finger back. *Oh no!* Sheila was unsure if she said this aloud or just in her head.

Did this motherfucker just threaten her? Or was he aiming at me? Really, you want to shoot me? He turned his body to the men and started walking towards them. The only sound was his heartbeat, thumping on his eardrums. The only sight was the enemy ahead. The only thought was...blood! Each blink, every breath delivered a different scene from a bloody place in his past. He saw Big O, unconscious, bleeding in the sand. He imagined Monkey Foot being murdered by Republican Guards and Big Greasy, shot by his ex. He saw Iraqi soldiers, shot, burned, blown apart. Iraqi civilians with dried blood stains, fresh blood marks, profusely spewing blood! He saw Big O's belly wound, Big O's right temple wound, and the large hole at the base of Big O's skull.

Then he saw himself kneeling down beside...**The One**. A large pool of dark red collected in the Iraqi's pant leg and the ground beneath. Painful cries and tearful prayers...he said, "Allah," many times...came from his mouth. Lowering his body closer to this man's face, Eiric's bayonet seemed a part of him as his fingers gripped tighter around the handle.

All of these images played in his head, as he rushed blindly into traffic. Four of the five men had moved to the sidewalk on the far side of the car. The man who had taken aim at Eiric, one of his restaurant assailants, remained on the street side, as Eiric ran directly at him. Car horns honked and drivers cursed as they slammed their brakes. Eiric didn't care, as he focused on the large, black, *Iraqi soldier,* standing beside a silver Grand Prix! Eiric launched himself off the ground and directed both feet at the man's mid-section. The soft belly easily pushed inwards, forcing his back against the car and all the air from his lungs. When Eiric's feet hit the ground, so did the big man. Eiric punched down hard on the space between his ear and the corner of his mouth and watched him slump to the pavement. He jerked his head toward the remaining *Iraqi platoon* standing on the sidewalk.

He ran around the rear of the parked car and rammed the closest *soldier*, knocking him and another to the concrete. One of them crawled backwards as he pummeled the ribs of the man underneath him. He paused as he felt a hand from behind, grab his shoulder. Eiric reached up, locked onto the man's wrist and gave a twist. He sharply leaned forward, reached up with his other hand, and flipped his attacker over him to the ground. Still maintaining his grip on the *Iraqi's* wrist, he stood and smashed his right foot down on the socket of the man's extended arm. A crunching noise was masked by the man's scream.

The crab-walking man, found his way upright and turned and fled the scene, but Eiric overtook and tackled him. Ignoring the stinging abrasions on his forearms, Eiric low-crawled on this man's back, punching, elbowing, and kneeing his way to his head. He grabbed a handful of hair and smashed his face on the ground.

The last *Iraqi* watched as his crew was being demolished by this much smaller man. He couldn't believe it was the same person he had urinated on last night. Eiric rose and turned towards the last man standing. A low, reverberating growl escaped him as he edged forward to meet the hulking figure. The large man looked in Eiric's eyes and instantly knew fear. With some effort, he raised his fists to protect himself but it was useless. Eiric ducked in and repeatedly punched his groin. As sharp, nauseating pain shot through the man's belly, he dropped to his knees. Eiric back-handed his face, then grabbed the neck of his shirt, half-choking him. His other fist jackhammered into his face, stopping only when he noticed blood bubbling and flowing freely from the man's nose.

He turned back to the clinic in time to see Sheila shake her head before disappearing inside. He carefully crossed the street, this time, and drove away. The other men helped each other into their ride and drove off the other direction. The police arrived long after the fight. There was no property damage or loss. There were no injured people present, and no suspects around. Too many conflicting eyewitness reports and no evidence of a crime led to a dropped case.

Outside the ice cream shop, Eiric reclined the driver's seat to wait for Gandhi's date to end. He decided against informing him about the fight. Even though he had won, Gandhi would be full of guilt for going against his own advice. He took his mind off fights and his friend and tried to remember his first kiss from Sheila. He imagined the two of them together, standing outside the clinic. He remembered how pretty she was even though she was upset with him and on the verge of crying before he made his move. Grabbing and kissing her was not part of his plan on his way over. At that moment, it just seemed like the right thing to do. The way she kissed him back, he was sure he did the right thing.

He remembered her soft lips, her sweet saliva mixed with salty tears, and the hint of her perfume. He squeezed his eyes tighter, forcing the experience to repeat, but he wanted more. He wanted to **live** the memory, like other thoughts that came to life in his mind. Comparing a memory to a flashback is like comparing a black and white photo to a big-budget, Hollywood blockbuster.

I want her back in my arms, kissing me again! Please! Why can't I have a flashback about good stuff, stuff I want to live through again? It's not fair! I can be minding my own business, and, Bam! There I am, going through that nightmare in Iraq all over again. Except, *it's not a nightmare or a dream, I feel like I'm **really there!** I can see their faces clear as day! I smell smoke from burning oil, metal, and burnt bodies! I hear the explosions from rifles, tanks, mines, and artillery and I can actually feel the shock waves! I get soaked with sweat thinking about the desert sun beaming down on us. How can I still hear voices from thousands of miles and several months away? Why can't anybody around me see what's going on? Why can't they hear it and feel it? Oh, yeah, because I'm crazy! Crazy Lesson! Shell-shocked Lesson! Why can't my craziness involve peace, love, or happiness? Why is it always about...Death?*

That question rolled around inside his skull for a while until he came to a dreadful conclusion. *Maybe I was supposed to die over there. Somehow, I cheated Death and now he's making me suffer for it. I guess, the only way to get rid of those thoughts is to give the Reaper what he feels he deserves. The way Sheila looked at me before she went back in the clinic, I'll probably never get another chance with her. Why did those clowns have to show up there? Why didn't I just get in this stupid car and leave? Why did I listen to Gandhi? She said she doesn't love me. After what I did, she never will. I should've just stayed at home and kept my big mouth shut. Maybe tomorrow, somebody will shut it for me.*

Gandhi opened the passenger door and slid in, laughing. "Dog, thank you for hooking us up! I am done with other females, she's the one! As soon as my enlistment is up, I'm coming back for her!" He watched her drive away, smiling back at him, then turned to Eiric. "E, you're gonna be my best man, when we...What the? What happened? Where did that blood come from? I knew I should've gone with you! Come on, Man, let's go to the ER..."

"Chill out! I'm alright!" He hadn't even noticed the blood on his hands or clothes on the drive over. "It's not my blood, so calm down!" As he drove to his parents' home, he told Gandhi about the fight. He told him that he ran into the men that jumped him in the restroom last night and he got payback. He didn't mention the fact that their numbers had grown. Gandhi was so wrapped up in thoughts about failing Eiric that he completely forgot about the ladies. He didn't ask about the meeting with Sheila and Eiric didn't bring it up either. He was too embarrassed to tell Gandhi that she wasn't in love.

At the house, they snuck inside. Eiric followed closely as Gandhi walked to the bedroom. Nobody noticed the blood, so Eiric was able to get to the bathroom to destroy the evidence. After cleaning himself, the phone rang, and he heard his sister calling for him to pick up. "I got it!" he yelled. He waited a few seconds before barking into the phone, "I got it!" He heard the click as his sister hung up the other extension. "Hello," he said, in a milder tone.

"Eiric?" He immediately recognized the accent and voice on the other side of the phone.

"Gabe? Hey, how you doing?"

"I'm ok. I was worried about you." Her English was almost perfect, and his German was okay, so they spoke in a mixture of English, German, and a little Turkish she had taught him. For over three years, this was the way they had always communicated. They talked about their families. They talked about their jobs. She wanted to know if everything was alright. He tried to assure her that he was fine, but she pressed on.

"You know I dream of you. Sometimes, when I'm awake, I see you. Something bad is with you, but I know that you won't say. I have a feeling I will never be able to see you again. Eiric, I don't want this! My wish is to be with you, here or there! But, when this is not possible, I want you safe. Tell me, there is no danger for you?"

He looked at the scrapes on his arms and knuckles, and said, "There's nothing wrong. Alles clar! I promise you, everything is fine." *She knows I'm lying!*

He was right. She knew he was hiding something. She didn't want to keep pressuring him, so she didn't stay on the line much longer. She held back tears as she whispered, "Ich liebe dich."

Eiric looked at the ceiling. Feeling she was looking right at him through the phone, he tried to escape her gaze. In a low voice, he said, "I love you, too," and hung up before anything else could be said. *How does she do that? Every time something bad is going down, she always knows. At least, I know she'll always be thinking about me.*

Across town, someone else had Eiric on his mind. Jerry was consumed with thoughts of him, as he sat in his room with his new best friends, alcohol, vitriol, and self-pity.

He took my job! He turned my daddy against me! The whole town is talking about him, and his Army buddy! 'Oooh, look at all his medals! Oooh, he's in the Army! He kicked Saddam's ass! Oh look, his friend is here to help him save us from the evil white people!' They can all go to hell, far as I'm concerned! He didn't do nothin' over there but hand out some band-aids! He didn't kill nobody! He ain't nothing but a cry-baby, bitching about seeing a bunch of dead people. They deserved to die! You don't fuck with the USA!

He took a drink and belched. *He ain't doing nothing now, except taking old folks to the doctor. They're paying him, no, **I'm** paying him to use an ambulance for a taxi. That could've been my job, but they had to hire* *somebody black. Blacks and Mexicans are taking all our jobs! Pretty soon, it's gone be their country, and we'll be their slaves! They're starting with the statue! That thang ain't bothered nobody, and ain't nobody bothered it, until now! Now, all of a sudden, it's got to go, 'cause it hurts Eiric's feelings? Wonder what he'll get rid of next? Let's see, you can't have white lines on the street, because they tell you what lane to stay in.* He swallowed more beer.

*Oh, yeah, we got to get rid of salt, 'cause it's white and it makes your blood pressure go up! What else? The White House! How could I forget that? We can't have that, we got to change the name and paint it, uh...rainbow colors! 'Then all y'all white people can leave the country, be **our** slaves, or die!' Yeah, that's what they want! Well, I ain't gone just sit around and let them niggers have it their way! I'm fixin' to do something about it! I don't know what, yet, but I'ma do something!*

He thought about how he had once been friends with Eiric. Now, he believed that their friendship was never real, that Eiric had been using him all this time. *Sneaky niggers! He*

*tricked me into being his friend! That's how he
got hired by EMS, they thought he liked white
people because of me! That nigger that's
rousing him up now, probably set the whole
thang up! That damn statue ain't never
bothered Eiric until that nigger showed up!
Why didn't I think of that before?*

He brought the bottle of beer to his lips and
tipped it for a swig, but it was empty. He raised
it above his gaping mouth, shaking it to make
sure nothing was left. He grunted then gingerly
lined it up on the coffee table, next to several
others just like it, before grabbing a new bottle.
He opened it and guzzled half the contents
before tearing it away from his mouth. He
spent the rest of the night in his dimly lit room,
drinking and humming to himself.

In Eiric's bedroom, Gandhi sat on the edge
of his bed shaking his head in response to
Gabe's phone call. "What did you do to that
girl? Man, you got a woman in Germany and a
woman right here going crazy over your crazy
ass! Come on E, look out for a Brother! Give
me your secrets so I can use them on Renee."

He stopped laughing when he saw the serious look on Eiric's face.

Uh, oh, I guess I said something wrong. I wasn't really thinking. He loves both of them. I better change the subject. "Yo, look outside! Your fire flies are back!" Eiric grunted. "I can't believe I was scared of some bugs last night. I had you ready to kill somebody!"

Eiric took a deep, noisy breath. "Everybody keeps asking me that. 'Did you kill anybody?' I keep telling everybody I didn't. Then they look at me like I should be ashamed of myself because I didn't. Man, I wouldn't want to live if I killed somebody. I pulled my M-16 on lots of people over there but I didn't pull the trigger. I almost did, twice, but I didn't shoot. I didn't kill anybody. That's what I keep telling myself.

"Honestly... I don't know! Sometimes, I think maybe I did kill somebody. I know I pulled a knife on a dude. I can see his face, like he's lying right here beside me. We stopped at the Aid Station, so I went to help with the wounded. My Man, Big O, was inside the tent being treated, but there were a few soldiers lying in the sand outside. I slung my rifle on my

back and squatted next to the man closest to
me. That's when I realized that these soldiers
were Iraqis. My dude was crying and praying, I
guess. He kept saying, 'Allah,' and a bunch of
gibberish I didn't understand. The pants over
his right thigh were ripped and blood poured
out of a few bullet holes. I put a large dressing
over the area and started pressing to stop the
bleeding. He screamed and grabbed one of my
forearms. He wasn't trying to stop me, he was
just hurt. Tears were flowing out of his eyes
and he kept calling on 'Allah,' so I told him he
would be alright. I tied the dressing tight. He
was shot in the leg, it was pretty bad, but he
was gonna be alright.

"I remembered Big O was inside the tent
with two holes in his head. He was having
trouble breathing and he had shit himself. He
was probably not gonna make it, but this dude
was gonna be alright. My Boy, that I was afraid
to help, was dying, but this Iraqi I was taking
care of was gonna be alright. This sorry
Republican Guard, that probably shot Big O,
was gonna be alright, thanks to me."

Eiric was sobbing now and engorged veins threatened to burst through his skin as he clutched his bedsheet. His skin glistened as sweat streamed from every pore. Gandhi's back stiffened as Eiric's voice changed to a low growl. "I said you're gonna be alright. You stinkin' raghead! Stop that fuckin' crying, you're gonna be alright. Big O was shot in the head, but I didn't hear him crying. You just got shot in the leg and listen to you cryin' like a bitch. My Boy is in there dying because of one of your boys. Or was it you? You shot him, didn't you? Say 'Allah,' if it was you. I knew it. I knew it. What the hell am I doing helping you? You're the enemy. You killed O, but you want to live. You probably will, because this wound is nothing. We're gonna fix you right up. You're gonna be alright." He coarsely whispered, "I should kill you." Eiric was on his knees, talking to his mattress. Gandhi jumped when he screamed, "Stop that damn crying, you're gonna be alright!"

Eiric dropped to the floor with a loud thud, screaming and writhing in agony. Gandhi tried to leave the room but his path was blocked by

Eiric's family. They were standing in the doorway, horrified at the sight of Eiric's battle with invisible demons.

"What happened?" demanded Eiric's father.

"I don't know! One minute he was talking to me about people bugging him, wanting to know if he killed anybody, then the next minute he was...he was...it was like he was talking to somebody else! His voice was...different!"

Eiric rolled in the sand, struggling to get another soldier, Private Smithey, off his chest. He was pinned down for some unknown reason. Maybe it had something to do with the bayonet in his right hand. Both his hands were bloody, but he didn't know why. The Major was yelling at him, ordering him to get away from his Aid Station.

What is he talking about? SmitDog, why are you sitting on me? I'm 'Baby Doc,' I'm here to help. Why am I holding my bayonet?

The man sitting on his chest stood over him and reached out a hand, helping him to his feet. Everyone else outside the Aid Station wore solemn faces and stayed their distance from him. Eiric turned towards the Scout Humvee, his feet shuffling in the sand in the last minutes of daylight. Over the sounds of gunfire and explosions, he heard a faint voice calling out to his God in a foreign tongue. Eiric wiped blood from his knife on his camouflaged pants before walking away. In his bedroom, his family watched as he patted his fist back and forth on his pajama pants before slumping to the floor.

The next morning, warm, bright sunrays on his face, stirred Eiric from a peaceful slumber. He blinked and rubbed away eye crust as his vision slowly adjusted. *Man, I don't remember going to sleep down here. Did I fall off the bed? Where is Gandhi?* His friend's bed was empty. Eiric pulled himself up after a satisfying stretch and made his way to the front of the house. Gandhi was half-asleep on the couch. "What's up, Bruh? Was I snoring?"

Gandhi deliberately struggled to put on his glasses as he tried to process Eiric's question. *Not again! He can't remember what happened last night! Bruh, you need help.* "You weren't snoring. I just couldn't get to sleep. Thinking about serious crap...that might happen today."

"Nothing bad is gonna happen! We're going to assemble peacefully, cops will be there, and the sun is shining! If some crazy shit starts to jump off, we pack up and beat feet! Cool?"

"Bet!" Gandhi was relieved to hear his friend making sense. It was a welcome change from the scene he witnessed last night. They got ready and promised to look for Eiric's family when they arrived. Eiric's parents hugged and kissed both of them before they left the safety of the house. It made Eiric think back to the day he left home for the Army. He had thought the same thing back then. *I may never see them, again.* He shook off that feeling as he walked away from them. He didn't look at them standing in the doorway as he settled in and brought the car's engine to life.

Crowds were already forming near the monument, so Eiric and Gandhi parked a few blocks away. They stepped onto the pavement, like two gunslingers headed for a showdown. On one sidewalk, an angry mob of white people, carrying signs supporting the statue, faced and yelled across the street at an equally angry throng of black people, holding posters protesting the slab of marble and yelling back from their walkway.

Cops on foot patrolled each side of the street, ensuring each side stayed put. Late-comers arrived and assessed which side they belonged on. Some people attracted even more menacing looks, if that was possible, as they crossed over to the 'other' side.

The "gunslingers," armed with rented mega-phones and petitions, approached the base of the statue. A familiar cop, Officer Lewis, approached them and asked for their permit. He looked it over and returned it after finding everything in order. "Well, looks like you get your parade, Mr. Hero!"

Eiric braced himself and quietly spoke. "You know, everybody's been calling me that and thanking me for my service. I didn't do anything that another soldier wouldn't have done, so I'm not looking for any parades. That was me doing my job. Nobody will care about me or the war a month from now. But you know what? Today I'm doing something I hope people will thank me for years from now.

Hopefully, today will be remembered forever. Thanks for being here to protect us, Office-Sir!" He turned to face the crowds. All of the yelling was now directed at them.

"Who do you think you are? That's our statue, Boy!"

"Go 'head! Tear that damn thang down!"

"Y'all can't take away my hair-tage! Y'all ain't got nuthin' in you don't want nobody else to have nuthin'!"

"Preach, Young Bloods! Let's show them what Black Power really means!" This voice, Eiric recognized. It was Trey, the nurse Earl had warned him about. "And if words don't work, we've got hammers, axes, guns...we'll help you tear it down, by any means necessary!"

"Why don't y'all just go on home and let that statue be! It ain't hurting anybody! The Civil Rights movement ended a long time ago! Git on, now!"

Gandhi raised the speaker to his mouth. Screeching feedback silenced the crowds so he could speak. "Sorry about that. I don't know who yelled that, but I'm here to tell you the movement never ended. It's still going strong and we're still here, in your face! As long as racial hatred continues to thrive and monuments built to highlight white supremacy continue to stand, the movement goes on! I'm not from here, but I see the pain in the eyes of every black face that looks up at this statue as he stares down on us. I felt my best friend's embarrassment when he realized I had seen this monstrosity up close and personal. His shame was tangible as he was forced to admit that something like this," pointing to the statue, "could never exist in my New York."

"Go back to where y'all came from and take him with you! We don't need your kind stirring up problems here!"

"They ain't going nowhere! The only one leaving is that Redneck on the horse!"

Eiric placed a hand on Gandhi's shoulder then raised it over his head. He looked over at the EMS building, where several paramedics leaned against the outer walls, spying from a distance. He pulled his own mic up to speak.

"Listen people! My name is Eiric Lesson, and I'm not going anywhere! I'm from here, lived here all my life, except while I was away.

Most of you either know me or my family or you know about us. I went to the Army, not to fight a war, but to get money for college so I could come home and help this town that I love so much. I've been all over the world, but this is the only place I ever wanted to live. Murfsburg. People think I'm crazy because I want to live and work and die in this little town, where you can still see shadows of slavery everywhere you look! We still have public restrooms with 'Whites' and 'Coloreds' painted over with thin layers of cheap paint. We have restaurants that have side and back entrances that Blacks are still forced to use, not by law but by years of, 'That's just the way it is.'

"We have schools that give passing grades and parades for minority athletes, but after they leave high school, nobody will hire them because they can't read. Meanwhile, the minority students that focus on their grades face ridicule in school for trying to be white, but when they leave high school, nobody will hire them because they're black.

"Nowhere is the division more prominent than right here. Right here, in the heart of this city. We all, White, Black, Brown, Red, Yellow, Purple...honestly hate this thing in the middle of the street. When we're late for work, we hate having to slow down as we approach this. When two or more cars reach the round-about at the same time, we hate trying to figure out who has the right of way. When we're stuck in traffic and can't get home because somebody has wrecked here because they couldn't figure it out, we hate whoever had the bright idea to put this here in the middle of the main street!"

Eiric could see people on both sides of the street nod in agreement. "The only time people express love for this obstacle, is when somebody of color has the audacity to question its existence. Then, and only then, does this obstructing, menacing, pigeon-magnet begin to gather disciples ready to kill or be killed to protect it from harm!"

Clamor began to rise on all sides as people were affected by his words. A shrill voice carried over the others, straining to be heard. "Damn skippy!" Eiric's eyes scanned the wall of people to his right. Finally, a well-dressed scarecrow of a man stepped out into the street to approach him. Eiric couldn't contain his joy as he recognized Skip, here in Murfsburg. He looked over at Gandhi, who smiled and signaled with his right thumb and pinky that he had called Skip. Eiric motioned for Skippy to join them but his friend was abruptly pushed back onto the sidewalk by a nearby policeman. There was no malice in the cop's action. He was just following orders, trying to protect the speakers at the circle. The crowds saw it differently.

Cheers rose from the left side of the street, where the statue's supporters congregated. Obviously, this black man was breaking the law, so the cop acted to protect the peace.

On the right side, where Skip was pushed back into the crowd, boos filled the air. Obviously, this black man was exercising his right, so the cop acted to protect *their* peace. Nobody noticed a single pickup truck a block away.

Jerry had made his way through the barricades unnoticed. All the focus was down the street at the round-about. Empty beer bottles rattled against each other as they rolled on the floorboard. He peered at the statue in the distance through blood shot eyes. He didn't know or care if it was lack of sleep, high blood pressure, or drunkenness that caused the fire in his eyes. He rubbed at the burning orbs with the back of his hand, but this only made it worse.

"Damn you, Eiric! You ruined my life, now you're making me go blind! Fuck you and that New York nigger!" Jerry slammed the last swallow of beer and let the bottle drop to join his brothers. He stomped his right foot down on the accelerator and the truck lurched forward.

Gandhi walked toward Skip, begging the crowds to stay calm. He had called Skip and told him about the bathroom fight and Skip promised to drop everything to be here today. He couldn't bear the thought of seeing his friend beaten by a policeman. Feeling responsible for bringing him here, he tried to direct attention to himself. He informed everyone that Skip was a famous author, here only for moral support. He tried to thank the police for doing a good job, but he was cut off by cries of, "Sell out!" A rock sailed through the air and bloodied his face.

The police began to wonder if they had enough backup to control the crowds. Gandhi dropped to his knees, but held up his fingers, telling Eiric he was ok. A woman, Jazz, pushed past Skippy to help Gandhi. Eiric's family tried to get closer to help Gandhi, but there were just too many people and they dared not step onto the pavement. Skippy also gave Eiric the Horseman salute. Eiric forced a smile atop clenched jaws. He was fighting shoulder pains that crept up as Gandhi was hit. With great effort, he raised the mouthpiece and yelled to the audience.

"ENOUGH! ENOUGH! ENOUGH!" The high-pitched squeal from the microphone helped him distract them. "I give up! My two best friends are here to help me, help us...do what? We just wanted to talk about removing this stupid statue. Maybe even beg for another statue to honor my ancestors who helped build this country. But if one person gets hurt, or worse, is it worth it?" He pointed at the statue.

"This is nothing but a hunk of stone. It has no feelings, it has no cares! We're fighting each other over a ROCK!" He stepped off the island of flowers and stood in the street facing Ol' Reb. "I'm tired of wasting my life hating you! You're nothing! The people who hold you dear worship a false god! I don't have to honor you by driving around you! I can choose a different road. We all can!

"Everyone who is offended by this Ol' Rebel, find another road that takes you away from his glare. Find a road that takes you away from those who will continue to serve him. Find a road that takes you to other businesses that don't fall under his shadow. We can raise the money to build our own statue in a place where people willingly go to see it, and not be forced to pay homage to this unworthy idol. Ol' Reb, I promised to bring you down someday, but I'm breaking that promise. Stay here as long as you like. From this day on, for me, you no longer exist!"

A woman's scream spun him around. Jerry's pickup was speeding towards him. Inside the truck, Jerry was laughing as he bee-lined to run down Gandhi. He was sure that he was the man holding the bullhorn in front of the statue. *Eiric is an Oreo. He ain't got the balls! That New York nigger is pulling his strings!*

As he drew closer, he saw Eiric spin around to face him. Jerry's maniacal grin dissolved as he recognized his old friend. He jerked his right foot to step on the brake, but something was preventing the pedal from moving. He glanced down at a beer bottle wedged between the brake pedal and the floor board. He looked up again at Eiric's face.

Eiric looked at Jerry in the cab of his truck. He noticed him looking down and then quickly back up. The engine roared as the truck closed the distance. Eiric closed his eyes and waited for the impact. He felt the kisses of Gabe and Sheila. He saw the Horsemen, trashing his room. His family sat at their kitchen table, offering him plates of food. Big O smiled and waved to him.

His family and friends at the statue screamed as he was hit. Eiric's feet flew off the ground as the blunt forced knocked the breath form his lungs. He heard the crunch of metal against stone, as the truck came to an abrupt halt. The pain he felt was surprisingly tolerable.

This must be Death. This is how all Combat Medics die in the movies. They get to have a final speech before the end. Damn! I can't think of anything clever!

He felt pressure on his chest and a crawling sensation on his torso and guessed it was his body ripping apart, like the disemboweled Iraqi he watched crawling in the sand. He looked up and saw the faces of the horse and rider he had come to destroy. They were moving towards him. Eiric inhaled a ragged breath, and then slowly closed his eyes.

"Move!" Eiric's eyes popped open at the sound of the man's voice. A cop was crawling over him, scrambling to his feet, as he tried to lift the man he had just tackled. Bewildered, Eiric could only back-pedal as the policeman grabbed his shirt. The pickup had crashed into the statue, barely missing Eiric and the cop who had saved him. The statue broke into hundreds of jagged pieces, falling to the ground as the truck's engine played a tortured dirge.

Eiric recognized his hero right away. It was the same cop, Officer Lewis, who had mocked a man in need and harassed him over a "missing" license plate. Eiric sluggishly came to realize this man, who hated him, had risked his own life for his. He reached out and firmly shook his hand. He suddenly remembered the friend that tried to kill him.

Most people scattered when the pickup crashed. Some stayed and scrambled to get the man out of the truck, but panic drove them away as smoke began to build. Eiric looked at the stalled pickup, smelled the smoke, and instantly had a brief flash of burning armored vehicles and smoldering skeletons. He saw Big O, bleeding in the sand, dying, as he uselessly stared, paralyzed by fear for his own safety.

He heard himself mutter, "Can't see through tears," before he screamed, "Jerry!" and ran to the truck. Jerry was not moving, so it was unclear if he was simply unconscious or dead. It didn't matter. Eiric had to get him out. The door was jammed shut. The only way in or out was the windows. Eiric grabbed a piece of the broken statue and smashed the rear window.

Gandhi and Lewis jumped on the bed of the truck trying to break out the small shards as Skip ran up to help.

"The seat belt is still on him! We need to get inside!"

"We need to hurry before this thing blows!" the cop ordered.

Gandhi yelled out, "Skippy!" The smaller man jumped up beside him and ripped off his overcoat. They placed it over the ledge of the windshield and Skippy crawled inside. He moved swiftly, unbuckling the seatbelt. Jerry's face was pressed into the steering wheel. Bloody bubbles formed at his nostrils as he exhaled. Jerry moaned as Skippy pushed the man's body back. He looked down and noticed his legs were partially pinned. There was no way they could pull him through the back window.

He shook his head, looking grimly at Eiric outside the driver's door. Eiric wailed as he frantically pulled at the door. Skippy positioned himself so he could kick the driver's door.

There was a glimmer of hope as the door began to budge. Gandhi and the policeman joined Eiric and yanked as Skippy used both legs to kick. The door gave way.

There was just enough room to squeeze Jerry's legs past the crumpled dash board. Eiric placed his arms under his thighs and snatched Jerry out. Lewis caught his upper body and they carried him to safety, several feet away. Gandhi grabbed Skippy's legs and yanked as hard as he could. Skippy skid across the seat and hit the ground running beside Gandhi. Expecting an explosion behind them, they both dove to the ground beside the other men.

Suddenly, Earl appeared at the truck. He aimed the nozzle of a fire extinguisher at the truck's engine. Billowing white clouds obscured his face as he pulled the trigger and swept side to side. He whistled a tune as he slowly, surely put out the flames. He winked at them as he strolled up to them. "Good work, Boys! And I don't mean nothin' racial when I say 'Boys,' all rat?" Nobody disagreed with the older man.

They all laughed as Eiric's family made their way to the men huddled around Jerry. They

encircled the men on the ground and praised
God for their safety.

The Final Word

"Well, here we are again, saying good-bye," Eiric stated. The three men stood in the middle of a park, gathered around a roped-off mound of dirt.

"Not, 'Good-bye,' how about, 'Until we meet again?' Remember, I'm moving back here to marry Renee. Renee Portland. It has a nice ring to it, right?"

"You don't care that I've seen her in the nude?" Eiric nervously asked.

"Nope! She doesn't mind that you've seen me naked in the showers, either! We already set a date. Besides, E, you need somebody to watch your back."

Skippy corrected him. "Gandhi, **we've** got his back! Horsemen...Forever! I just wish Greasy was here. Ok, I'm not gonna cry, 'cause he wouldn't want to see that. You know, that giant knucklehead only wanted everybody around him to be happy. As big and menacing as he appeared, he never hurt anyone. He didn't deserve what happened to him. No soldier should die like that! I hate that I wasn't there when he needed me. I hope you both know I'm always there if you need me."

"We know, Skip. You were right on-time when I called you about E. Plus, you saved us from begging and scraping for money."

Eiric smiled, "Yeah, Bruh, you really came through! Greasy would love this. I talked to the artist this morning. He said the statue should be ready in about two months. We're gonna place it right here in the center of the park. Four slaves, bound by friendship, helping each other survive! That's what **we** did over there in Germany. Y'all helped me survive. I used that picture of the four of us in Munich as the model for the statue."

"I can't wait to see it. We had a good time that day. Wasn't that where you met Gabe?" Skip asked.

"Hell no! He was already with her! This buster had her meet us there so he could look like a player! You fell for that, Skipper? I have to admit, it was a smooth plan."

"Wait a minute, Gandhi! How did you know?" Eiric was once again blown away by his friend's mystic powers.

"I'll say it again. You're the dumbest genius I know! I asked Gabe if you two knew each other. Too much coincidence, Bruh! Anyway, Gabe's in the past, now that you have Sheila!" He shook his finger at Eiric as they walked to their cars. Skippy had a rental car, so he was taking Gandhi to the airport. He was going to Los Vegas for another book signing. Gandhi was ready to return to Germany, so he was wearing his dress greens. Eiric didn't envy the long trip ahead of Gandhi, but he was a little jealous of the looks his friend got as they left the park. He rubbed his palm against one of the new brick columns that supported a towering sign.

They paused to read the name on the arched entrance: Specialist Alfred "Big Greasy" Reynolds Memorial Park. The citizens of Murfsburg didn't know who Greasy was, but nobody complained. All they knew or cared about was that the park was paid for by someone else and it was dedicated to a soldier. The three men gave their Horsemen salute and turned to the parking lot.

Skippy broke the silence. "You know, I really like Sheila. Don't mess up with her or I might have to steal her from you."

"Naw, we're cool. We're taking it slow. We're having lunch with Renee, Jazz, and her friend tomorrow, but I'm seeing her tonight. Man, I thought I lost her a couple of times. First, when I got beat up, then, at the rally after she heard about Jerry almost killing us both. I'm glad that fool is ok, but me and him are through. Oh, yeah, I almost forgot, I almost lost Sheila when I went crazy on those dudes outside her clinic."

Skip raised his eyebrows at Gandhi then hugged Eiric. He got in the car as Gandhi cleared his throat. "Look, Eiric, you and this skinny knucklehead are my family. I love you, Man. I **am** moving here when I'm done overseas. Promise me something. Promise me you'll get some help." Eiric rolled his eyes and started to turn away. "E, you're not crazy, but you need help! Don't go to those military quacks if you don't trust them, but please, go somewhere and talk to somebody. You know you can always call me or Skippy, but I need you to see a professional. For me and Skip, for Sheila, your family, Greasy, but most of all, do it for you. We can't afford to lose another Horseman. I would really miss your brain!"

"Ok, I promise." Gandhi looked skeptical as they shook hands. "I promise! Now get outta here before you miss your flight." They hugged and patted each other on the back before Gandhi joined Skip in the rental. As they drove away, Eiric raised a fist and yelled, "Horsemen...Forever!"

He got in his own car and slammed the door. He watched the car carrying his best friends until it disappeared beyond the curve in the road. *He knew I was lying. There's no way I'm gonna go spill my guts to civilian Soft-Talkers! I'm all right. I can deal with stupid dreams on my own.* He looked at the reflection of the archway in his rearview mirror and fought a stinging sensation in his eyes. *Can't see through tears! Can't see through tears!*

It was his mantra during battle, when fear became his closest companion. He knew it would remain with him the rest of his life. Suddenly, the faces of the dead, the cries of the wounded, the sights, sounds, and smells of destruction flooded his senses. For a moment, he thought about the pistol in the trunk of his car. It was so close.

He shook his head and all these thoughts faded away. A vision of him and Sheila holding hands slowly developed. He started the car and drove home.

On his way, he drove past the new flower garden in the round-about in the center of the main street. The fragmented base of the former Civil War monument had been dug up a day ago. Accompanied by a small convoy of mourners and a police escort, the irreparable chunks of stone, pebbles, and dust had been hauled away to the local dump.

As he drove the car slowly past, Eiric smiled and whispered to the pedestrians gathered at the circle, "That's right! I brought Ol' Reb down, just like I promised! You're welcome."

Tyrone R. Gibbs, Jr., better known as, "Tony," to his family and close friends, grew up in a small town in NC. He joined the US Army after high school as a medic with dreams of being a doctor one day. He was deployed to Saudi Arabia with his unit, the 4/64th Armor Battalion, Scout Platoon, as part of the 24th Infantry Division at the start of Operation Desert Storm. In 1991, Desert Storm became Desert Shield, as combat began in Iraq to free Kuwait. He was awarded the Combat Medic Badge and the Bronze Star Medal. After completing his active duty contract, Tony continued to serve in the Army Reserves. His civilian life included working as an EMT, a dialysis Patient Care Technician, and going to nursing school fulltime. He is currently an RN and Home Hemodialysis Program Manager in TX.

Tony began writing this story, piecing together journal entries from his Gulf deployment, as a way to explain his mood swings, pain, and tears to his family. The story took an unexpected turn, as he found himself fighting racism as well as his inner demons. Despite finding writing to be therapeutic, this story was put on hold several times as he dealt with these, and other, negative issues. After years of, "Handling this on my own," he listened to the advice of friends and family and began receiving help with PTSD at the VA Hospital. He no longer suffers in silence and encourages others to seek the help they need. Tony continues to enjoy writing poems, stories for children, and other genres.

73811505R00196

Made in the USA
Middletown, DE
18 May 2018